She stepped clos them. "Ben, I w

He was drowning in the pools of her eyes and clenched his jaw shut as the hairs on the back of his neck stood up with the remembered comments from Julia. *Yeah, you want me, but only because you hadn't found anything better, right?* Anger flared and he narrowed his eyes, adding aloud, "Your parents should have named you *Jezebel*."

"What?" Her eyebrows rose as confusion clouded her eyes. She blinked. "I know this looks bad, but I can explain."

He ignored the plea in her voice, put the hat on his head and swallowed. He took a step backward as she came forward.

"Ben, please listen." Her voice trembled. "I can explain. I want you—"

He put his hands on her shoulders to prevent her from coming any closer, but as soon as his palms touched her skin, his hands started shaking. Something was wrong, different, he could see it in her eyes. And the way she looked? This couldn't be the same angel his heart had longed for—had everyone else really seen what he couldn't?

"I don't want to hear it. I already know," he snapped, delving into his self-loathing and fortifying his resolve. "You stole my hat—a hat I was going to give my little brother."

"No, that's not how it was." Alex pressed against his hands and tried to move in closer, her eyes rimmed in tears.

Praise for Christine Columbus

CHRISTMAS MISCHIEF:
"Ms. Columbus writes with such humor. I was cracking up with Charlie's innocent antics and feeling so sorry for Amber not having the easiest of times trying to get to Grandma's house. I love Ms. Columbus' writing style and I look forward to reading more stories from her. You will not be disappointed if you pick this one up for yourself."
~Night Owl Romance

"*COFFEE AND LOVE TO GO* is a sweet story about the beginning of a relationship. Christine Columbus hits a nerve with the two shy characters that need help coming together. They find it with help from a radio talk show. *COFFEE AND LOVE TO GO* is a must read. My only regret is it didn't last long enough. I look forward to reading more by Christine Columbus."
~Tracey, Fallen Angels (A Recommended Read)

UNCLE MIKE'S LOVE:
"Ms. Columbus' tone is realism with a heart. This story is too good to put down until the reader finishes. The author should take pity on her fans and add a remote control with a pause button for those moments when life interrupts reading her delicious stories."
~Jade Taylor, Harlequin Superromance

The Perfect Country and Western Story

by

Christine Columbus

The Perfect Country and Western Story

Cover Art by *Tamra Westberry*

The Wild Rose Press
PO Box 706
Adams Basin, NY 14410-0706
Visit us at www.thewildrosepress.com

Publishing History
First Yellow Rose Edition, 2010
Print ISBN 1-60154-659-9

Published in the United States of America

Dedication

For Michelle Barton,
Ashley, Bridget, Michelle and Sandy Fyle
for helping me plot out the story at WE Fest.

For Patty Columbus,
my sister-in-law, friend, teacher and mentor,
for reading and editing the story,
and my friends and family
who continually support and help with suggestions:
Rich Herbst, Sarah Shock, Colleen Rowland,
Pat Freiheit, Mary Manke, Toni Riley, Sandy Dzik,
Mike White and Kortney Haag.

For my editor, Stacy,
who never gave up on me or the story,
and has patience and insight.

For Rhonda and RJ
who created a place for writers to bloom.

And for Bridget and Isaac
who have always believed in me.

Chapter One

Where is she?

Alexandra Coe pulled a cell phone from her white denim skirt pocket. She paced across her driveway and checked the time again. Almost ten. Eyes shielded from the morning sun, she glanced down the street.

"My goodness, is that you Alexandra?" Mrs. Henderson's head of tight white curls bobbed behind the white picket fence next door. "I almost didn't recognize you all dolled up."

Alex waved and offered the nosy neighbor a toothy grin just as a red Focus raced up to the curb.

"See ya," she called out and jogged to the street. When Shellie Lindberg stepped from the car Alex breathed a sigh of relief. "Finally!"

Shellie latched onto her shoulders. "Who are you?"

"Real funny. Come on we have to get—"

"Seriously. You sound like Alex, but the hair, make-up...oh my gosh, a pedicure!" Shellie slapped her hands on her cheeks. "Who are you and what have you done with my grease monkey friend?"

Alex grinned. "It's good to see you, too."

"Is that Shellie?" The elderly neighbor cackled.

"Hello," Shellie shouted over Alex's shoulder.

She jumped back, her hand cupping the side of her head. "That was my ear you screamed into."

Her best friend laughed and took a step toward the fence. Alex grabbed onto her arm. "Come on, we're in a hurry. You can chat with Mrs. Henderson when we get back."

"Don't be silly. This will only take a second." Shellie side-armed Alex and continued to the fence.

Mrs. Henderson's age-spotted hand reached over and rested on Shellie's forearm. "Don't see much of you anymore, just Alexandra tinkering on her car."

Alex stopped two feet from the fence, crossed her arms and tapped her foot. They didn't have time for this. "If your car is unlocked I'll start packing," Alex suggested.

Shellie turned and held up a finger. "One minute. I'll be right there." Her friend turned back to the neighbor. "Do you see that—the tomboy polished and pretty? Who would have thought beneath the grease and coveralls was a beauty."

Mrs. Henderson's head bobbed vigorously. "It's a shame her mother isn't here to see her now, like a butterfly from a cocoon. Just last summer I told her mother not to worry..."

Alex tossed up her arms. The two of them talked about her like she couldn't hear. A breeze caressed the back of her legs and she quickly pulled on the edge of her short skirt.

"Oh my, look at the time." Shellie pointed to her watch. "We've got to get going. We're on our way up to Country Time to find our new beauty queen her cowboy."

Heat rushed from Alex's puckered stomach to her face. "You can stop talking about me anytime now."

"It was nice talking to you, Mrs. H." Her friend laughed. "Come on."

Alex yanked on Shellie's arm. "Me come on? *You* come on. I've been waiting all morning—no, make that *all year* for this."

The fine blond hairs on Alex's forearms quivered with excitement at thoughts of corralling her cowboy. She smiled as her feet glided over to her restored '69 blue Mustang convertible. She unlocked the trunk. For a whole year, she had been waiting for this weekend, and for the past two weeks, every thought had been on the possibility of seeing Ben again.

The time has come. Her stomach dropped to her knees as they headed back down the driveway to her friend's car. Just imagining his brown eyes and the feel of his strong arms had her licking her lips in anticipation of a kiss.

She turned toward Shellie and fanned herself with a hand. "One minute I'm hot, the next cold. It's crazy. For two weeks I haven't been able to think straight." Images of Ben headlined all her dreams, leaving her oversized night-shirt tangled around her body. Sometimes she woke up glowing, with bits and pieces of the previous night's dream floating back to her during the day.

"It's love," Shellie said.

Alex gave her friend a shove. "Seriously, I think I'm going crazy. One moment I'm cranking on a wrench, and the next I'm staring into space."

"Infatuation, lust, love it doesn't matter, always starts out that way. The rush of feelings crowding out everything else, the only thing that matters is seeing him again and then bam! You break up and you think you'll never smile again and then someone else comes along." Shellie winked.

Alex rubbed at the chill crawling up her arm and nodded. Yeah, that's how it was some nights. The dreams weren't so pleasant and she'd wake up in a cold sweat with the words, *"please wait,"* caught in her throat. Shivering, she brushed the goosebumps from her forearms.

Her best friend's boisterous voice scattered the nightmares to the wind. "Remember how excited you were last year to win those one day passes to Country Time to see Toby Keith? You were talking so fast, I had no idea what you'd won." Shellie jumped up and down in an animated portrayal of that day.

Her cheeks warmed and Alex gave her friend a shove as they moved alongside her Focus. "Knock it off. Besides, it was the first time I'd ever won *anything.*"

Shellie popped open her trunk. "You're a little sensitive today."

She ignored her friend and pulled out the cooler. When you'd spent your life feeling like an outsider and a loser, well, being a sudden winner caused a person to do odd things.

Shellie grabbed a couple of bags and a backpack then headed back up the driveway. She put her sleeping bag in Alexandra's backseat. "And remember you didn't have a thing to wear to the show, so I picked up that little black-knit dress for you."

"As I recall, it was *you* who said I didn't have anything to wear. I would have been content in cut-offs and a T-shirt." The truth was, she hadn't worn anything but jeans since kindergarten. She hadn't been too impressed when her best friend showed up at her door with a big grin and a shopping bag from a ladies' wear boutique. Not wanting to hurt her feelings, she'd gone to her bedroom to change. When the black knit slid over her skin, however, she couldn't help feeling like Cinderella. The transformation was amazing—and if she had to pick one moment that just might have been the start of her desire to have it all—mechanical talent, scraped knuckles, fitted, flattering clothing, beautiful nails, make-up *and* love—that would have been it.

She warmed at the memory. *From an ugly duckling to a swan.* Yesterday, oil-stained, worn, chipped nails, covered in grime, adorned her fingers. Today, red, sexy, shapely acrylic ones danced when she wiggled them. The change left her speechless and feeling sexy.

Speaking of sexy, the cool satin of her thong slid between her waxed legs as she set some things down next to the Mustang. Alex grinned; she could get use to the new her.

"I do love the nails. Red is a great color for you." Shellie's smile turned crooked, like she had bitten into something and couldn't decide if she should spit it out or swallow. "I'm trying something new, too. I stopped by Wal-Mart and bought...a *thong*." The last word eked out on a whisper.

Alex placed a perfectly manicured hand against her cheek, and mouthed the word, *No*. For once, she was one up on Shellie. She laughed at her friend's red-tinged cheeks and pulled a pink, Victoria's Secret gift bag from the front seat of her car. "I was going to save this for later, but since you brought the subject up..."

"Oh!" Shellie tucked her brown hair behind her ears and grabbed the present. Her hand slipped between the sheets of pink tissue paper, and she cautiously pulled out the black, Chantal Thomass pleated lace bra with hot pink ribbons and bows. Her eyebrows shot up to her hairline as she held the bra away from her as if it was road kill.

"It won't bite," Alex said on a hardy chuckle. "It's a bra. Here let me hold it." She grinned and took the bra from her fingertips. "There's more."

Shellie chewed on her bottom lip and reached deeper into the bag. If possible, her eyes grew wider. Pinched between her thumb and forefinger, she pulled out a matching see-thru thong for a half-second before she quickly dropped the panties back into the pink package, grabbed the bra from Alex and trapped the intimate apparel at the bottom of the bag.

"I, ummm..." She clasped the top of the gift

while chewing her bottom lip and fanned herself with the bag. "Wow, it's really sexy." Shellie opened the bag again and peered inside, brushing the tissue paper aside. "Like, I mean, hot, *really hot*. I'm not even sure I'll know how to put it on." She cinched the bag shut again, her face deepening to rich crimson. "You really didn't have to buy me anything."

"I know, but I wanted to." She gave her long-time friend a big hug. "You deserve something extra special. You've been my lifeline this past year. I don't know what I would have done without you." She gave her hand an extra squeeze and added, "And we're going to Country Time!"

"Yee haw," Shellie hollered, tucking her present in the back seat with the rest of her gear.

"It's hard to believe it was just a year ago," Alex said. "So much has changed."

The one thing that hadn't changed was their friendship. Inseparable through high school, Shellie had been the sister she never had.

Her friend yawned.

"Tired?"

Shellie shook her head. "Nope, long drive and not enough coffee."

Alex's eyebrow rose. "Sure it wasn't a late night with...what's his name? Bill?"

"No, but it *is* a three hour drive to your house. Do you have any idea what time I had to get up to get here on time? Besides the fact, I still had to pack."

Alexandra intentionally hip checked her. "Who's the sensitive one now?"

She pulled the remaining gear from Shellie's car, barely managing to wedge the oversized bag next to the tent. The site of the recent tattoo of a heart on her upper arm caught her eye, and she let her gaze gently trace the word, *Mother*, written on the inside.

"You have everything?"

Her father's deep tenor drew her gaze away from past sorrows. A few feet away, he navigated the recently installed ramp from the house. Brenda, his new lady-friend, watched protectively from the front screen door.

A year ago it had been her mother standing by her father's side waving good bye. Her chest tightened and her father's recent words echoed in her head. *If wishes were pennies I'd sell everything I own in the hopes of bringing your mother back, but wishes are only whispers into the wind. She'd want us to move on, to continue to live. Your mom wanted us to be happy. Life is precious; we've learned that the hard way. When you meet someone new, you don't have to discard what is in your heart—your mother's love is gold, Brenda's is silver and I have room for both.*

Alexandra blinked back a tear. The time had come to break out of the cocoon that had become her life. Her dad was moving on with his life and she would too. *Life is precious; we've learned that the hard way.* He was right. And this weekend was going to be the on-ramp to the expressway of life; from now on, if she had the chance to sit it out or dance, she was damn well going to start dancing! She *was* going to have it all.

"Ow," she rubbed the spot where the wheelchair bumped her leg. "It's a good thing you didn't need to pass a test to drive that thing."

"I couldn't have possibly hit you. You were a million miles away," he joked.

"Funny." Out of habit, she pulled a blue bandana from her back pocket and tied up her light brown mass of hair.

"So, you got everything?"

She caught a glimpse of the cooler filled with beer, the Victoria Secret Bag and the brown paper

7

bag with the bottle of Jack Daniels hidden inside. "Uh, yeah we...um..."

Her father narrowed one eye and shook his head in disbelief. "Honey, you're twenty-five. Just don't drink and drive, be careful and *try and have some fun.*"

"Don't worry, Mr. Coe." Shellie jabbed Alex in the ribs with her elbow. "I'll make sure Alex tears it up a bit."

A smile creased his face. "That'll be the day." His voice turned gruff. "Girl Scouts have more fun than you two."

"Girl Scouts?" Alex rolled her eyes. When her gaze landed back on her dad, her jovial mood turned to concern. "Are you sure you'll be okay?"

"Don't worry about me." A twinkle came into her father's eyes as his voice boomed. "With you gone, I can finally have my own wild party."

She chuckled, bent down and placed a quick kiss on his cheek, so happy to see his sense of humor and desire for fun coming back. He was looking for love again, too, and she hoped he had found it. Someday he'd probably have another wife, but there would never be another mother for Alex. No one would fuss over her and tell her she worked too hard, or she needed to get an office job where she could meet a nice young man.

At that moment, a beautiful Monarch butterfly spread its wings and fluttered by. Alex could almost hear a sweet voice say, *Butterflies carry messages from heaven* and *you won't find your man sitting at home.* Echoes of her mother's words lifted her spirits.

"Now you two get into that car," her father ordered. Alex quickly slid onto the black vinyl bucket seat as he wheeled up to her window. "You girls have a wonderful time. Do you have the cowboy hat?"

She glanced at the tan Stetson perched on the

middle console. Alex traced her finger over Toby Keith's signature. "Right here."

"I hope you find him." Her dad's voice trailed off as he wheeled himself up the ramp.

Stunned at her father's remark, Alexandra turned wide eyes to Shellie. "I guess he wasn't asleep all those nights when you and I sat up talking in his hospital room."

Shellie giggled. "Guess not."

Their eyes met and they shrugged simultaneously. Alex was certain Shellie was wondering about everything else they had said, too.

She waved goodbye to her father as she turned the key.

"Need any sunscreen?" her friend asked.

"No...but what are *you* doing?" Alex turned in time to see Shellie smear a gob of sunscreen on her nose, then pull out mirrored sunglasses.

"Whenever I wear these my nose burns."

Alexandra grabbed her own sunglasses from the dash. "Maybe you should try a pair that isn't mirrored." Not to mention they made her look like a giant bug.

"But these are sooo cool. All the celebrities wear them."

Alex hid her grin as she backed out of the driveway. "Who would have thought I'd be driving off with a Hollywood starlet," she smirked, maneuvering around the corner and giving one last wave to Mrs. Henderson.

She shifted gears and wondered for the millionth time if this was nothing but a wild goose chase. A smile pulled at her lips. *No, a wild cowboy chase.* One that would take her back to the old Dude Ranch, the venue for Country Time for more than twenty years.

Each year in Minnesota, the sleepy little town of nine thousand transformed into a community of over fifty thousand country fans who gathered on the grassy fields for a weekend of music, camping and partying.

As if reading her mind, Shellie stuck her elbow out the window, leaned back and said, "Don't worry. We'll find him."

Alex smiled. "You're right. How hard could it be to find a cowboy amongst fifty thousand people, seven campsites and in only three nights?"

"If he's there, we'll find him. And if not, we'll still get to listen to some great country music."

Not wanting to think about that possibility, she teased, "And maybe we'll even find someone for you to show off your new apparel to."

Shellie sat straight up, her arm no longer resting on the window. "Alex! This weekend isn't about me. It's about you and finding your cowboy. If I happen to run across someone, well, maybe I could let him in on a little Victoria's Secret."

"That would be a first, meeting a guy and asking him to help put on your bra and thong." Alex laughed and a finger jabbed into her arm.

"Of course I know how to put on a thong, I was only teasing. Humph, just because you no longer shop at Wal-Mart." Shellie's voice dropped down to a level just below a shout. "I bet you never even went in the store, just ordered it all online."

Her chest expanded. She knew her way around an auto parts store and a tool chest, but when it came to her feminine apparel, she had been out of her realm.

Alex adjusted the bandana on her head. "Filling out the application for school and registering for college was a snap compared to getting the courage to walk into the store. My face was beat red and I thought for sure everyone was staring at me and whispering, 'Look at the girl here to buy an outfit to trap a man.'"

Shellie laughed. "Honestly you come up with the craziest ideas. Everyone knows it isn't wrappers, it's the package that men are interested in."

"Good thing I didn't think of buying bras and thongs as wrapping paper or I might have never gone in."

"Well, if Ben's half the man you say he is the wrapper won't make any difference." The starlet's mirrored glasses flashed in the sunlight.

"Hmmmm, he is."

A hand brushed her arm and brought Alex back to the moment.

"So, what did you buy?"

"I had no idea there were so many different types of bras." Alex pulled up the end of her shirt to reveal her new favorite, a lime green, push-up bra. "Cool, huh?"

"I didn't think I'd ever see the day when you bought anything other then a white sports bra. I feel faint." Her best buddy attempted a dramatic gesture of wiping her brow, but only succeeded in smearing her sunscreen.

Alex rolled her eyes. "You goof."

Shellie poked her side. "Seriously though? I wasn't sure that was you when I pulled up to the curb. You really have changed."

"I'm trying to re-make my image. I don't want to be forever known as Bud's grease-monkey daughter." For years, she had tried to be the son he never had. But with the loss of his legs came the freedom to change. During his recovery and rehabilitation, they had plenty of time to talk. The moment she remembered the most was when he had reached for her hand and told her the garage had been his dream and he had no regrets, but wanted her to find her own life and her own dreams.

Her red nails flashed as she adjusted the mirror and checked out her complexion. She grinned, knowing she was going to put another one over on Shellie. "You should have seen the look on Rebecca Nelson's face when I made an appointment for a beauty make-over."

Shellie bolted upright. "*You* went into Nelson's Day Spa and Beauty Bastion?"

"Yep." Alex smiled smugly. "Had my eyebrows waxed, a facial with make-up consultation and a massage. I was there for the *whole* day."

"Did you get a bikini wax?" Hollywood crossed her legs, scratched her chest and squirmed in her seat. "I bought one of those kits."

"And how did that go?"

"Duct tape would have been less painful."

A laugh rushed from her lungs. "I never know what you're going to say next." From the corner of her eye, she watched as Shellie examined her slowly.

"You have changed."

She reached up and adjusted her bandana. "I know. I feel the same on the inside, but when I look in the mirror, I can't help but wonder who it is looking back."

Hollywood adjusted her glasses. "Looking at you now, no one would ever imagine in high school you preferred to spend all your time under the hood of a boy's car instead of in his back seat."

"I would have loved for a boy to invite me into the backseat, but as soon as the conversation veered from fuel injectors, belts and plugs I became so tongue-tied I couldn't swallow."

The starlet squirmed and adjusted her bra. "With the exception of Larry." She slid her glasses up, smearing the sunscreen onto the lenses.

"Speaking of Larry, I ran into him when I went out to dinner with my dad and Brenda last week."

"I still can't believe you liked him." Hollywood made a gagging sound. "All junior year you followed him around like a puppy on a string. He was skinny, with acne, and those ugly glasses." She shuddered. "You acted like he was a movie star. There was no talking to you. Then he spends the summer with his dad out in California, comes back to school with contacts, a clear completion *and* an attitude."

"I know. All through senior year he wouldn't even say 'Hello' to me. I was heart broken; he was my first love."

Shellie glared at her. "You never told me that. If I had known I would have busted him in the nose, or at the very least spit all over his Girl Scout cookies."

Alex glanced into the rearview mirror and grinned. "I wish you could have seen the look on his face last weekend, though. I swear his mouth hit the ground and all he could babble was, *'you're so hot'*."

"Serves the loser right—"

Alex shrugged. "Actually, he's done quite well for himself. He's into real estate now."

From the corner of her eye she saw Hollywood peering over the top of her sunglasses. "Don't tell me you're still interested in him?"

"Nah, he's married. But he did make my dad an offer on the Swifty Oil Change Shop."

Her friend slid the glasses back up her nose and settled into her seat. "Please tell me he married Tina, she's gained a ton of weight, all her hair fell out and her boobs sag to her knees."

"He did marry Tina...and she's not as pretty as she once was."

"Yes!" Hollywood whooped as she sat upright.

"She's even *more* gorgeous." Alex tried to hide her smile.

The starlet swooned then sat up, her expression frowning. "Wait! Back up. Your dad is going to sell the shop?"

"Yes, I think he is. And, for the record, Tina has put on a few pounds."

Shellie folded her hands in prayer as she tipped

her head up at the sky. "Thank you."

"Don't tell me there is a patron Saint of ugly."

"If there was, I would have been prom queen." Shellie cocked her head, looking anything but regal.

Alex laughed as her friend scratched her chest again, reached over and turned the radio on. Toby Keith's, *Don't Leave, I Think I Love You,* roared from the speakers.

Tingles rushed through her as thoughts of Ben once again spread their wings. Warmth wiggled up from the pit of her stomach and her hand fluttered to her chest. Last year, everything had been so easy. Alongside her cowboy, her words flowed easily from her mouth, and they had talked for hours. When Ben took her in his arms, they fell right into step. "That's the last song Ben and I danced to," she sighed.

"I wished I would have been with you to see him." Shellie crossed her arms against her chest and pouted. "Instead I wasted my time looking for Jim."

Alex blinked as images from last year flooded her mind. Ben's hands slid down her black jersey dress, the soft material clung in all the right places, and when they danced, her black spaghetti strap slowly slipped off her shoulder. He'd bent low, and his warm lips traced her suntan line.

Her breath caught and a shiver went up her spine. Unconsciously, Alex picked up Ben's hat, her smile bitter sweet. Before the song had ended that night, Ben had taken his tan Stetson and placed it on her head. She could still smell his scent, a combination of virile man, sunshine and cold crisp nights.

Shellie's fingers brushed her forearm. "We're going to find Ben, I just know it."

Alex grimaced. "What if he thinks I just ran off with his hat and hates me?" She put the Stetson back down. "Or worse, has a girlfriend...or a wife." Old insecurities and fears had her second-guessing her decision to find Ben. "Let's face it. I've never been the girl that got the guy. I didn't even get Larry."

"The *old* you didn't get Larry. The new you will have every guy saying, "Wow!" The hair, the make-up—"

Sudden whistles and hollers punctuated Shellie's words and Alex whipped her head to the left. Alongside on the interstate was a pick-up truck with four gorgeous men, two of whom were waving cowboy hats at them. The bed of the truck behind was loaded down with camping gear.

"See you up there, darlin's," one of them called out, right before the driver gunned it.

"I. Told. You." Shellie emphasized each word with a poke to her arm.

Alex sat up taller as she caught the cowboy hotties' fun-loving, carefree attitude. "Save a dance for me," she shouted.

She fell back in her seat, grinning ear to ear.

Hollywood pushed her glasses down and peered over at Alex. "I heard on the radio that tickets for Saturday are sold out." She reached up and tipped the rearview mirror in her direction, applying more sunscreen. "Ben might be hard to recognize."

Alex brushed the starlet's hand away and readjusted her mirror. "Don't worry. I remember every detail of him. His faded blue jeans clung to his narrow hips, tan muscular arms contrasted with his crisp white shirt." *His butt beneath his shirttail so muscular and taunt.* Her tongue traced her lips as his had. "The way the brim of his cowboy hat shaded his mocha brown eyes, the shadow of his beard, the confident, broadened shoulders and his deep, sensual voice vibrant when he spoke..."

Her friend sighed loudly. "You're giving me goose bumps."

"I know. Sometimes I think I could jump start a

car just by touching my finger to the battery terminal." Her smile grew as *She Said Yes* by Brad Paisley drifted over the airwaves.

"Do you believe in fate?" Shellie asked after he sang the line in the song.

Alex turned up the radio. "As in, was it fate that brought Ben and I together, or was it fate that separated us?"

Shellie turned the volume down. "Well?"

"Maybe. I guess," she stuttered. "I mean, if the phone call had come five minutes earlier. If Ben wouldn't have left or put the hat on my head. If there never was an accident..." Her grip on the steering wheel tightened. *It wasn't fair.*

"I'm sorry." Shellie's fingers brushed her forearm. "I didn't mean that it was fate to have your mom killed or your dad wheelchair bound."

"I know," Alex murmured, wondering for the millionth time why her mom had to die.

"I'll never forget that drive to the hospital. I remember wishing my car went faster. We had no idea if your dad was going to live or..."

"I know."

Alex's thoughts wrestled with her past memories. She always thought about her parents' accident and Ben with a kaleidoscope of emotions. Ben's arms around her, swaying to the music, wishing the moment would never end; it was the happiest she had ever been.

And the absolute worst moment of my life. She knew because the precise moment was engraved on the death certificate. She'd been dancing on Earth, while her mom took her first steps in Heaven.

Alex pinched the bridge of her nose and swallowed hard.

Shellie's hand rested heavily on her shoulder. "Maybe it's all too soon."

She shifted her thoughts to the present. "No,

Mom would want me to be happy. I have to put my life in order, to have no regrets. I don't want to spend my life reminiscing, wondering if I'd let 'The One' get away."

Her best friend's hand slid from her shoulder.

"Besides, I think my dad has plans for Brenda this weekend that don't include his adult daughter hanging around." She attempted a weak smile.

Hollywood's head tipped back as a burst of laughter rushed out. "Your dad did have a big grin on his face when you backed out of the driveway." She gave a disgruntled smirk. "Well, at least someone's going to get lucky."

"Don't make it sound like you're the one who never had a boyfriend. Not that I've been counting, Snow White, but you've dated *seven* guys so far this year."

Shellie smacked her forehead with her hand. "Now I get it. When I was going out with Jim you referred to him as Dopey and Tom was Grumpy and you kept calling Bill, Happy."

"Oh, I liked him! Whatever happened to Happy?"

Alex changed the radio station, and glanced over to see why the sudden silence in answer to her question. Face beet red, the starlet sat slack jawed, acting like she suddenly forgot her lines.

"Oh, now you *have to* tell me."

Tangled brown curls swished left to right, picking up speed as her lips pinched tighter.

"Come on, we're best friends."

Hollywood's head slowed and color came back to her released lips. She leaned closer. "I don't know if I can tell you."

The only spot on Shellie that wasn't red was her sunscreen-slathered nose. *Oh this should be good!*

Shellie's mouth popped open, closed, opened and closed.

17

"Quit with the imitation of a goldfish and tell me."

A small smile parted her friend's face. "Oh, all right. Two weeks ago, Bill called and we decided to go play bingo at Jimmie's Bar and Grill. Remember I told you that I won a hundred dollars."

"You broke up because you won?"

"No."

"Well…" Alex gestured with her hand.

"I didn't realize Bill had already been drinking when I picked him up. He seemed fine. We got our cards and our daubers."

"Daubers?"

"Bingo daubers. You know those markers with sponge tops." Her right hand closed into a fist and she tapped out a rhythm on her left palm. "You use them to blot out the numbers on your bingo card."

"Oh yeah, daubers." Alex imitated a bobble head doll. "Sure, everyone knows what a dauber is."

"Do you want me to tell you or not?"

"Sorry. Go ahead."

"I had on a white T-shirt. We were sitting on bar stools at a pub table over by the windows…"

Alex turned the radio down further to hear.

"When the game started, there were three cards on a sheet of paper and we each had our own sheets. After the third number was called, I looked over and Bill was just staring at me. He hadn't even daubed his free spots." She poked her finger into her outstretched hand. "So I tell him, "Do your free spots." Then I twisted on my bar stool toward the TV so I could see what numbers he missed. All of a sudden, my nipple is cold and wet. I screamed. Before I could swivel back around I screamed again. My *other* nipple's wet and cold." She crossed her arms over her breasts. "I looked down and here Bill had daubed my boobs."

Alex barely suppressed a giggle. "I guess he got

those free spots." A belly laugh broke loose and she held harder to the wheel. She swiped at the tears sliding underneath her sunglasses and rolling down her cheeks. "He actually daubed you?"

Hollywood crossed her arms, mouth set in annoyance. "Yes. Bright blue blobs right over my nipples. Everyone stared at me when I ran to the bathroom."

"Did it ruin your shirt?"

"No. It washed right out of the shirt, but my nipples were stained. Then when I tried to scrub the dye off, I got a rash."

She tried to keep her lips from splitting into a wide, open-mouthed grin, but failed. "Well, that explains the scratching. I thought maybe you were wearing a new bra and had forgotten to take the tags off."

"Just forget the whole thing, okay. We're on a mission for you...not me." Shellie tossed the tangled hair from her shoulders, stuck out her tongue and cranked up the tones to deafening.

"On the road again," she sang in a rising pitch. She put her feet on the dashboard and bellowed out, "Can't wait to be on the road again."

Alex dialed the radio down to loud and joined in for the chorus, itching to be in Ben's arms again.

Chapter Two

"Now how long?" Hollywood flopped on to her side in the seat, stretching out her arms and legs.

"We've just passed the three hour mark, so half hour, tops."

Alex chugged down what was left of her water. Her stomach churned. Her palms were sweaty on the steering wheel. In less than a half hour she might know the answer to her question. *Did Ben wait for me?*

"Oh man," Shellie bolted upright in her seat. "I completely forgot to ask. Did you hear from Kakato University?"

Her smile widen as she nodded. "As a matter of fact, I did."

"And?"

Grinning, Alex could barely hold in her pride. "I was accepted into their college of Science, Engineering and Technology."

"Congratulations! When do you start? Where are you going to live? How—"

"I found a cozy little apartment by the river to rent," she replied, drumming her fingers on the steering wheel as she talked.

"Are you nervous?"

"A little. At twenty-five I'll probably be the oldest person in class."

The starlet scratched her breast. "You'll be amazed at how many people go back to school."

"I know and it's time. I'm tired of barely scraping together a living changing oil in other people's cars—"

"Look, look!" Shellie interrupted, pointing excitedly to the Country Time billboard. "Turn left. Hayfield Camping is right over there."

Alex signaled and came to a stop behind a long line of trucks, trailers and cars waiting to get into the campground. Contentedly, she set her concerns about starting school aside and let Shellie play tour guide.

"Across that street over there and to the right is the family campground."

"Hopefully we won't find Ben there." Alex shuttered.

"Down a little further is the adult campsite, Lake Harriet. They were already sold out."

"What!" Alex jabbed her friend. "You told me we were staying in the adult site."

"Calm down. Hayfield is recommended for twenty-five to thirty-five year olds."

"Oh, thank God. I was afraid you'd booked us into the eighteen to twenty-one year old campground."

"No way. Definitely not into cradle robbing. Besides, they're too wild for me," Shellie said.

Alex tapped a fingernail on the steering wheel. "I know what you mean, I can't decide if they are really racy or they just have wild imaginations. When the teenagers are waiting for their oil changes, they talk like I can't hear. The things I've learned."

"It's hard to believe we were once that young." Shellie sat up, tugging the edges of her T-shirt.

"We're not that much older! It's just that we were never that adventurous is all."

Shellie folded her arms across her chest. "Speak for yourself. When I was a Girl Scout—"

"Oh right! You *were* a Girl Scout. Maybe you could work on earning a badge for being bold and racy this weekend," Alex joked.

"Shhhhh." Hollywood pressed a finger to her lips. "You'll ruin my image."

"Your image is a step below St. Theresa. I don't see how Girl Scouts could ruin it."

"Ever since Bill daubed me, everyone thinks I'm wild. I went to Karen's Kurls Wednesday for my sassy new cut"—Shellie's fingers puffed the wind blown mess—"and Edna, the eighty-year-old owner of the beauty shop, wanted to know if I was going to show my boobs for beads at Country Time this year."

Alex half-gasped, half-chuckled. "And what did you say?"

Shellie scratched her chest and laughed. "I asked how many strands she wanted me to bring her back."

A tired looking woman in her late thirties interrupted their hysterics. "I need your camping passes and driver licenses if you're over twenty-one."

Alex handed everything over.

A few minutes later, the woman came dragging back with a parking pass, blue wristbands that she securely attached around their wrists and recycle/garbage bags.

"We're new to this camping." Alex looked past the check-in point to the mass of campers haphazardly parked in what looked like an old pasture. "Do you have any idea where we should go?"

The woman peered into the backseat. "Just a tent, huh?"

Alex slid her sunglasses down and twisted around. "Yeah, just a tent. If we're lucky, maybe later we'll add a handsome cowboy."

The staid woman actually chuckled. "The cowboy might be easier to find than a camping spot. But if you take the gravel road all the way through the field, turn left and you'll see a smaller field. Go to the end and you'll come to a hill."

Alex nodded at the trees pointed out in the distance.

"The RV's can't make it up that steep hill. You might be able to find a place to squeeze in. Take the last right and see if you can find a place that backs up along the fence."

Shellie unbuckled her seatbelt and stood up, looking over the top of the windshield. "I didn't think it would be this crowded. The music doesn't start until tomorrow."

"The gates for camping opened up yesterday. We've already had almost eight hundred vehicles in Hayfield. By tomorrow, there'll be over twelve hundred."

"Wow." Alex shifted into first and Shellie sat back down. She eased the Mustang by trailers littered with crushed beer cans. "Looks like some of them have already been hitting the partying hard."

"Look over there, they have a wading pool. Oh, oh, can you believe it. A hot tub—"

"And look at that! A stripper's pole?" Alex asked, driving slowly through the camp area. "Do you think women really strip here?"

Shellie tapped on the bag in the backseat. "Well, if I get drunk enough, I've got just the bra and panties to do it in."

Alex chuckled, turned into the next field, took a left and headed up the hill into the wooded area. "I thought this was going to be like camping at the state park where everyone had a little campsite." There were tents, trucks and SUV's scattered throughout the trees. "Any ideas?"

"Let's ask him," Hollywood suggested, pointing to a twenty-something guy in a golf cart heading toward them.

"A sixty-nine?" he asked, outwardly admiring her Mustang.

Tufts of blond hair stuck out of a Twins baseball

cap and a barbeque-stained white T-shirt was tucked into stiff new blue jeans. Alex was just thankful the guy didn't have a belt buckle with his name on it.

She ran a hand across the dashboard. "Yep, a classic. Had to do a bit of work, but now she runs like a champ." Alex beamed as he smiled and nodded toward the interior.

"Sweet," he said.

"I know." She tapped the steering wheel. "There's something about a Mustang with a 351 under its hood."

"I was talking about you ladies." His smile grew. "Sweet...and just the two of you?"

Shellie nodded her head so exuberantly Alex didn't bother to respond.

"I've got just the spot. It's about half way down the road, a little past the port-a-potties. You can get your car far enough off the road and the ground's pretty flat for pitching your tent." He paused, listening to a broken voice crackle over his radio. "I've got to go, but if you need anything my name's Joe." He pulled the golf cart off the road so they could pass.

Alex saw the small clearing up ahead and pulled in. She wrinkled her nose. "Well, I guess it's not like we're going to spend much time here."

Shellie was twisted in the seat and looking backward. "Looks good to me."

"What looks good to you?"

"Did you see that guy? Wasn't he cute?"

"Joe in the golf cart?"

"Yeah," she sighed. "He was so nice and his eyes were a brilliant blue."

"Perfect. They'll match your boobies."

Hollywood made an unladylike gesture. "I knew I shouldn't have told you."

She tossed her sunglasses into her purse as Alex

parked next to a big maple tree and cautiously opened the door. She had spent over a year re-finishing the car and didn't want to ding the door on her first trip.

"Your cheeks are rosy." Shellie had been right about the reflective power of the sunglasses. Her nose wasn't red, but her cheeks were.

Hollywood hopped out of the car, twisted and bent to get a look in the side mirror. "Oh no! I look like a clown! And I still have white stuff on my nose. Joe probably thinks—"

"That you're hot."

Shellie's grimace turned to a grin. "You think so?"

While her friend daydreamed with a grin the size of Texas on her face, Alex pulled items from the backseat. "Hey, Hollywood." She tossed the nylon tent to Shellie. "Let's get our tent set up so we can walk around and maybe catch a glimpse of your leading man."

Shellie rolled her eyes and unzipped the bag.

Alex knelt down beside the pieces her friend dumped out. "Where are the directions?"

Her answer was a shrug.

"Come on, there has to be a picture or something?"

"I don't know. It's *your* tent." Shellie pushed the poles around with her toe.

"I borrowed it from old man Haley. He assured me everything was in the bag."

"Well, he lied to you because there are no directions." Hollywood turned the bag inside out. Only metal stakes and dirt tumbled to the ground.

Alex picked up the tent. "Oh well, how hard can it be?" She spread the canvas out and started snapping poles together. "A little help would be nice," she said, handing a couple stakes to Shellie. "It's a dome. We'll just push from the opposite side and then stick the stakes through the black tabs on the bottom."

"I don't know." Shellie fiddled with the poles in her hand. "You should have checked to make sure the instructions were in the bag. You should have done a trial run—"

"I'm the mechanic, remember? *You* were the Girl Scout. So start earning a badge and *push*," Alex barked out the order. When the tent popped up, she added, "Quick, put in the stakes."

Within minutes, her side was secured and she headed to another.

"I think this side is stuck."

Alex glared. "Put some muscle into it and pull."

"Ahhhhh. *Humph!*"

She raced to the other side to find Shellie spread out on her back, waving a piece of the tent in the air

"Need some help?"

Alex spun around to the front of the tent to find Joe climbing out of his golf cart.

"Can you sew?" This from Shellie who was still spread eagle with the black tab fluttering in front of her.

"No, but I can tape." He walked over and held out his hand to Shellie. "Here, let me help you up."

The starlet beamed brighter than the lights on Broadway as she put her hand into his. He easily pulled her to her feet, then bent down and duct-taped the tab to the corner of the tent.

"That should hold," he said, admiring his handy work.

Star-struck, Shellie rested her hand on his arm. "We don't have much, but could we offer you a beer? I put a six pack in the cooler. They should be cold."

"Unfortunately, I'm working." He stood straighter.

Not missing the subtle interaction, Alex watched Hollywood go from bright and perky to looking like a flower without water.

Joe nudged Shellie's foot with the toe of his shoe. "But, if you're offering a rain check, I'd love to stop by when I get done and see if you're around."

"Okay."

His grin was as big as Shellie's when he got back in the cart to go.

"See ya," he said, driving off.

Alex laughed. "Is that how you did it in the Girl Scouts?"

Preening, Shellie grinned. "Not exactly. First, there weren't any men—or beer."

Alex giggled as she and Shellie began to toss their stuff in the tent.

Before pulling the last item from the car, she plunked the cowboy hat on and heaved the cooler to the ground. "What did you put in this thing?" she asked, dragging it closer to the tent.

Shellie opened the lid. "Diet soda, bottled waters, beer, a couple wine coolers, candy bars with nuts—protein in case we get hungry—and salve for poison ivy. What do you want?"

"I don't want poison ivy, but I will take a diet soda."

"Sounds good."

She handed one to Alex and popped the top on her own. "Who knows, maybe next year it'll be you and Ben driving up here," Shellie said as they began walking along the edge of the gravel road.

The smile came with an energy surge and there wasn't a spot in her body that didn't tingle. "I wonder what Ben is doing right now?" Alex murmured aloud. "Do you think he's here? Do you think he remembers last year?"

Chapter Three

Ben Buck folded his arms and leaned against the fender of his truck as he watched Julia Shartan wheel her large red suitcase down the sidewalk. She sure looked hot in her white cotton blouse, matching skirt with high-heeled shoes and long red hair cascading down her back. She couldn't have been more than five feet tall with big blue eyes and bright red lips. There she stood, posed against her *way too big* suitcase, acting like a miss-priss china doll. Instead of walking to the truck, she strolled, swinging her hips as if every man on the street were watching.

His eyes rolled. She was definitely *not* his type. High maintenance was written all over her forehead. No doubt she was used to champagne and caviar and this weekend there would be nothing but brats 'n' beer.

He shook his head, wondering once again why he ever agreed to take her to the concert with him.

He turned and peered into the bed of his truck. Full. He scratched his head and tried to figure out how he was going to fit the oversized suitcase in. Ben dropped the tailgate and was rearranging the gear when his best friend Mike pulled up to the curb in front of Julia's house.

"Ready to go?" Mike asked.

"As soon as I find a spot for Julia's suitcase." Ben tried to keep the annoyance from his voice as he stacked the tent on top of the lawn chairs.

Julia grasped his arm as he shifted one of the

cases of beer. "I'm soooo excited," she bubbled. "I've never slept in a tent before."

Ben let a sigh escape. No doubt she'd be expecting him do all the work this weekend. Setting up the tent, fetching ice and wine coolers. He could already hear the whining, *Why are there so many bugs here? Is it always this dirty? Don't they have electricity?* He should have quickly declined last weekend at the softball tournament when Mike's wife, Laurie, used her charms—and half a case of beer—to get him to agree to take her co-worker, Julia, up to Country Time.

He turned to find Mike's eyes boring into him. The corners of his friend's mouth tipped up as if to say, 'I know what you're thinking, but if you know what's good for you, you'll be nice.'

There would be hell to pay if he tried ditching her now, so he kept his mouth shut.

"I just heard from Dan and Patrick," Mike volunteered. "They roped off an area big enough for all of us. The bad thing is the spot is by the entrance at Hayfield near all the RV's."

Ben shifted his eyes down to the sweet little thing attached to his arm. "I guess we'll be waking up to the sound of loud, smelly generators again."

She didn't even flinch at the news. Probably can't wait to meet our RV neighbors, sit under their awnings, sip Piña Coladas and say things like, 'You gotta get out and rough it once in awhile.'

Gingerly, he pried himself from her arm, glanced hopelessly at the suitcase and then at Mike. *You owe me,* Ben thought, straining to lift her suitcase. "What did you pack in here?"

She tilted her head and smiled. "Just the usual girl stuff."

"Definitely don't have to worry about your suitcase blowing out of the truck."

"Good thing." Her smile turned dangerously

sexy. "If my little nightie ended up spewed alongside the road, what would I wear?"

The hairs on his arm stood up and his eyes widened. The little filly might just end up being too hard to resist. His brows dropped when he spotted Mike and Laurie watching them. What *conspirators!* Those two wouldn't be happy until he was corralled and saddled with a woman. This weekend it was Julia, and if that didn't work out, by next weekend Laurie would be parading another distant cousin or long lost friend in front of him. *Would they never give up?*

Ben scuffed his heels in the dirt as he walked to Mike's red truck. Just as he figured, Laurie had a smirk on her face that wouldn't quit. The look in her eyes told him she was content playing matchmaker. Maybe there was still time to get out of this.

"Good morning, Laurie. A little under the weather?" Ben asked, noticing the coffee hugged tight between her hands.

Her blue eyes slitted and didn't hold the usual sparkle under heavy lids. "No. I worked the late shift. By the time I got home, packed, to bed..." She blinked, and all at once her eyes shone soft and dreamy towards her husband. "It was late."

Ben shook his head at the stupid grin Mike had plastered on his face. "I can't believe you two, looking all starry-eyed at each other. You're not even newlyweds anymore."

"Well, I think it's so romantic and sweet." Julia purred like a kitten.

It's contagious. Not only do women go to the bathroom in twos, they get all sentimental and romantic together as well.

All he needed was for Julia to read more into this weekend then there was. He'd have to set her straight so she'd know that he wasn't the relationship type. He knew nothing would make

Laurie happier than to see him settle down. Since Mike just wanted Laurie happy, he'd definitely be outnumbered this weekend. The muscles in his neck tightened.

A smile slid across his face like a knife through warm butter as he looked at the empty seat in their extended cab. "Maybe Julia would be more comfortable riding with you." He ignored the glare from Mike. "You know how you girls like to talk. Besides, you're all such good friends."

"Don't be silly," Julia cooed. "You and I are going to have sooo much fun."

He took a deep breath, his gaze lingering on her small, frail stature. She looked as fresh as a flower and he hated to be the one to make her wilt. "Julia, I'm not a morning guy," he began, his tone soft but firm. "I'm kind of crabby." The thought of being polite and nice for the five-hour drive had his stomach jumping like a colt being put out to pasture. He just wanted to turn up the radio and turn off his thoughts.

"I think I can put you in a better mood." She used her words like sugar cubes, tempting, coaxing—

The hairs on the back of his neck stood straight up. *I'm her personal challenge—it's written all over that pretty little face.* His nostrils flared. He was in a no-win situation.

Carefully, he detached the china doll with the kung fu grip from his arm. "Let's, uh, go then."

She walked over, standing poised and expectant at the passenger side door. "A gentleman always opens the door for a lady."

He walked to his side of the truck. Guilt churned in his galloping stomach as he defied everything his mama had taught him about manners. But he didn't have a choice. If he was a gentleman it would create expectations and at the end of the weekend she'd be disappointed. Best to nip it in the bud now.

He grinned at her little pout as she climbed in. "It's not too late to change your mind. I'm afraid I won't be very good company," he added hopefully.

She crawled into the passenger seat, flashing her cleavage.

"It's okay. Laurie told me all about last year when some bitch stole your cowboy hat and broke your heart."

His brows shot up as his mouth popped opened. He didn't know what surprised him more, Laurie blabbing about last summer or those words coming from the sweet little mouth next to him.

"Don't tell me you never heard a lady say the 'B' word before?" Casually, she pulled her long red hair back behind her neck and fastened it with an ornate silver and turquoise clip before pinning him with a wicked stare. "And just so you won't be shocked, I've also tossed out the 'F' word a time or two."

His foul mood flew out the window as a chuckle slipped between his parted lips. From the corner of his eye he gave his cab partner another glance and a shake of his head. Ben grinned, started the truck and turned up the radio. Just his luck, Toby Keith's *Don't Leave, I Think I Love You* roared from the speakers.

Why did that song have to play now?

The smile faded from his lips as he glared at the radio, not sure who he was angrier with, Toby Keith for singing the song at Country Time last year in the first place, or himself for thinking that the green-eyed woman had been *'The One'*.

She had been a siren, calling to him in the little black dress that clung in all the right places. As the material slipped off her shoulder, his lips rushed to kiss her suntan line. He suddenly felt the weight of a thousand horses standing on his chest. *How could I have been so stupid?* He had asked himself that question a million times over the past year and still didn't have an answer.

"Hey, cowboy, you look a million miles away." Her warm, soft fingers brushed his arm. "Let me guess, that was your song?"

He gave a slight nod, and didn't try to stop her when she boldly changed the station.

"I know how you feel. Last month the asshole I was dating kicked me to the curb. He's an attorney and met up with the daughter of a senior partner from a prestigious East Coast firm. One minute it was 'I love you' and the next it was 'See ya later.'"

His tongue stuck to the roof of his mouth. He pulled a pack of fruity gum from the ashtray.

It wasn't just that his autographed hat had been stolen, but that the beauty had made him look a fool in front of his friends. He thought she was perfect, so he left for only half a moment to tell them about her. When he came back, the good-looking woman had vanished...along with his hat.

Ben popped the whole stick of gum into his mouth and greedily chewed until the inside of his cheek was drenched in the sticky sweetness.

"You still want her," Julia stated flatly.

He shook his head vehemently and waved the package of gum at her. "Want some?"

"If the only thing you're offering is gum, the answer is no."

"Sorry, that's all there is."

The tips of her fingers moved slowly from his knee to his thigh before fanning out and searing his leg.

"Well, cowboy, if you change your mind, you know where to find me."

She squeezed his leg, leaving her hand draped on his thigh as she leaned back in the seat and closed her eyes.

Ben spit his gum out the window and reached

for another piece as he tried desperately to distance his thoughts from the hand caressing his thigh. *Damn!* If he wasn't careful, she'd have him rode and broke before they got to Country Time.

Her hand dropped to his crotch and he felt warmth in more than his leg. He slid her hand slowly back to his knee where he hoped it might stay.

The corners of her mouth twitched. Her eyelids fluttered. "You don't have to be shy."

"And you don't have to be in a rush. It's a five hour drive."

"Mmmm, I think I'm going to enjoy this ride."

The corners of his mouth twitched and the weight of his chest shifted slightly. She was pretty, spunky and definitely a distraction. He grinned. She might be just what he needed to get through this weekend. "It just might be my pleasure, ma'am."

****

When they pulled into the campsite, Ben was wound tighter than a drum and in desperate need of a cold shower. Julia had the smile of a Cheshire cat.

Finally out of the tight confines of the truck, he called out greetings to half-a-dozen men, and accepted a cold beer from Patrick. "Where's your tent?"

His softball teammate nodded to the left. "Wasn't much of a choice, but I'm downwind from the generators and upwind from the porta-potties."

Ben nodded and popped the top on his beer. He drank half down, knowing it would do little to cool the fire burning in the pit of his stomach.

Patrick slapped Ben on the back. "Quite a looker you brought with you." His eyes were planted on Julia and Laurie as they walked down the gravel road.

"Want to bet he loses her like he did the hat?" Mike said, joining them.

"Real funny." Ben shoved him his beer. "Hang on to this until I get the tent set up."

He scanned the area then pulled the canvas from his truck and dropped it on the ground next to Mike and Laurie's.

"Hey," Mike complained. "What are you doing?"

"What does it look like I'm doing?"

"There's more room by Patrick."

"I like this spot better." Ben pulled the nylon tent from the bag and began inserting the poles.

"Come on," Mike said. "If you got any closer, we'd be in the same tent."

Ben ignored his friend and finished putting in the stakes before dragging Julia's suitcase out of his truck and dumping it inside. Next, he took his belongings and walked toward Patrick's tent.

"What's the deal?" Patrick called out. "You're not putting your stuff in my tent."

"I'm bunking with you."

"No way." His teammate ran and blocked the entrance to his tent. "This is *my* love shack."

"If I crawl into the tent with Julia, Laurie will be planning our wedding by Monday."

Patrick slid the baby blue bandana he wore like a pirate cap down lower on his forehead. "All right, then put Julia's stuff in my tent."

"Knock it off." Mike pushed Patrick from the entrance, nodding toward the women who were only fifty feet from them.

Ben dropped his bags, his eyes narrowed at Mike. "This is all *your* fault."

Mike handed him back the beer. "I'll make it up to you. After I get back with some ice."

"Sure." Ben turned his back, stepped over his sleeping bag and walked toward their group playing washer toss around the fire pit. He joined in the game, thankful for the distraction of good-natured teasing that came with each missed point.

Laurie plopped—and Julia swooned—into lawn chairs ten feet from the game.

"Hey Ben," Julia called.

Patrick's elbow nudged him. "Better go trot off and see what she wants." His voice was low and barely audible, but not low enough that the other guys didn't hear.

They chuckled; Ben glared.

"I hope you didn't give her the keys to your truck," Rick, another teammate, said.

"Ben, honey. Ben?" Julia's voice was a pitch higher.

"Run, Ben, run," Patrick teased.

Ben glared at each of the men. "Knock it off," he mouthed the words more than he said them.

"I know," Rick said. "Maybe she wants to bring you into the tent and play your own game of ring toss."

More chuckles followed.

"Ben, honey, please come here," Julia cooed.

If Mike wasn't his best friend, and if he hadn't been Mike's best man, he'd pick his tent up and camp somewhere else.

"Oh Ben, come quick, come now," Julia moaned loudly.

The men were outright belly laughing. Laurie's cheeks were beat red and everyone stared at him. Wasn't much he could do but grin and bare it, so he stood and strutted over.

"Would you be a hon and grab me a cold beer." Julia said.

Ben's arms folded across his chest. He needed to put an end to this now or she'd have him running ragged by the end of the weekend. "If all you're asking is for me to be your servant or lap dog this weekend—"

Patrick started barking, rushed to the cooler, trotted over to Julia and handed her a beer. "I'll be your junk yard dog."

"Hmmmm," Julia reached out and scratched Patrick's tummy. "Would I be able to teach you some new tricks?"

Patrick's tongue fell out of his mouth. He panted 'yes.'

Ben rolled his eyes. This was going to be a *lo-o-ong* weekend.

Mike strode into camp. "I'm not even going to ask, but if you're done drooling over Julia, I'd appreciate it if you'd open the coolers so I can dump the ice in."

"Aye, aye, Captain," Patrick said.

When the last of the ice covered the brews, Mike walked over to Ben, looking like he found all the answers to life's mysteries.

"What?" Ben asked.

Mike shrugged.

"Come on. You know something. Did you find a place we can get ice for free?"

Patrick walked closer. "With a grin like that, it would have to be free beer."

What's up with him? Mike acted like a woman with a secret and ready to burst at the seams.

"When I was getting ice," he began, grin confident and annoying. "A ground worker pulls up in a golf cart and told the clerk about two hot babes in a blue, '69 convertible Mustang. One of them was named Alex."

As if kicked by a horse, Ben staggered back a step. "She's here."

"I don't know if she's your Alex, but—"

It had to be her; last year she mentioned the '69 Mustang she'd been restoring. Ben ran his hands through his hair. "An Alex with a '69 Mustang... what are the odds?"

With an annoying smile, Patrick ran his finger and thumb over the stubble on his chin. "You still got a thing for her."

Ben stopped pacing. "A thing for her? No, she's got a *thing* for me. And it's called *my hat*." His hands clenched the air and his boots kicked up dust. "The beauty played me like a rodeo clown." He stood toe to toe with Patrick. "And I'll tell you something. When I see her, it won't be my lips I'll want to wrap around her neck this year."

Patrick slapped Ben on the shoulder. "Hey man, let me grab my guitar. I'll sing you an updated version of the perfect country and western song with a '69 blue Mustang, stolen cowboy hat and a big, broken heart."

Mike nudged Ben. "Yeah, instead of Mamma, trains and prison, you could have—"

Ben pushed the two of them away. "I don't even know why I hang out with you two."

He stomped past the tents to the gravel road, glancing past the large motor homes.

A slap landed on his back and a beer in his hand.

"Come on. Let's take a walk and see if we can find her," Mike offered.

He nodded, but before he got three steps down the gravel road Julia ran up and wrapped her arms around him.

"Don't leave me," she wailed.

His eyes dropped to the redhead wrapped around his waist. His hand brushed the top of her hair. "It's okay." He softened his words as if he were talking to his younger brother instead of a beautiful woman. "I won't be gone lo—"

Her wicked green eyes flashed as she threw back her head with laughter. "Lighten up and give me a kiss, cowboy."

Besides spunky, she was crazy, the exact opposite of Alex. And maybe exactly what he needed—

"The cowboy won't kiss you," Patrick's voice boomed as he plucked a guitar string and continued to sing. *"Haven't been able to kiss a gal, since I gave my heart and hat awa-a-ay..."*

Ben scooped up Julia, kissing her as he twirled her around, putting on a good show for Patrick and hoping to make Alex's memory fade.

Julia's legs wrapped around his waist and a cheer went up from the crowd. When his boots stopped turning, she slowly slid down his body, fingers still clutching his shirt as her feet hit the ground.

He glanced over her head to the singing pirate who laughed and set down the guitar.

Julia flattened her hands across Ben's chest, fingers playing with the buttons. "Do you need any help tracking the bitch down?"

His body stiffened and his brows dropped dangerously low. "If I had any soap, I'd have to wash out that potty mouth of yours. Didn't your mama ever tell you that ladies don't swear?"

Her hands slipped around his waist. "Cowboy, I'm no lady." She slapped his butt. "When you're done exorcising your demon, come find me and I'll prove it."

"Yeah," he mumbled.

She popped up on her tippy toes and planted a loud, wet kiss on his lips. "I'll wait...but not too long."

"Hey, Patrick," Mike hollered as the kiss ended. "You coming with?"

"Only if Julia will kiss *me* good bye." Patrick adjusted his bandana, his focus on the redhead.

As Julia swayed past Patrick, her finger brushed across his lip. "Sorry, pirate. I'm only kissing cowboys this weekend."

Patrick tugged the stubble on his chin. "You say that now, but wait until I put on an eye patch and make you walk the plank."

Ben turned from the show. "Let's go."

"Are you sure?"

"Yes. Let's go find my hat."

"So then," Mike began. "What else can you tell me about the elusive Alex, besides she had green eyes and brown hair?"

"She's wearing my tan Stetson," Ben grunted, nodding a greeting as they passed fellow campers.

A guy in a ratty Viking's T-shirt held up a tray of red Jell-O shots and called out a generic greeting. "Hey, step right up. Only a couple more minutes before power-hour is over."

The ground was littered with abandoned plastic containers and the crowd was jubilant as they shouted in unison. "Five."

Ben plucked a plastic glass from the tray—he could use a shot after Julia's theatrics.

"Four."

His voiced blended in with the crowd. "Three...two...one. Bottoms up."

Plastic cups crinkled, crackled and dropped to the ground as the tray went around again and Ben and Mike took another shot.

In sixty seconds it began all over again. "Five...four...three...two...one. Bottoms up."

Ben was feeling a bit better and even laughing by the fifth and final round. After crushing his last cup, he elbowed Mike. "Good thing we didn't get here any earlier."

Mike nodded. "Laurie would kill me if I came back drunk."

He shook everyone's hand and thanked them. When someone offered him a beer, he turned it down. "Now that I've had a little fortification, I'm all set to find that woman."

"Don't you mean *fornication*?" a man with a 'P' painted across his bare chest called out.

With a shake of his head, Mike laughed. "That's what Ben *should* have done. Instead, he'd let the lady walk away with the hat he had signed by *Toby Keith*."

A fine looking gal in a tight tank top and pigtails gasped as a cougar in a short black skirt and tight white T-shirt walked over, her smoky blue eyes traveling the length of Ben. "What does she look like?"

"Brown hair, green eyes, about this tall." Ben held his hand to the tip of his nose. He raised a brow as the cougar gave him a smile and a wink.

A few feet ahead, a man in a faded purple shirt and cut-off sweat pants bellowed, "That'll be as easy as looking for"—the man laughed so hard his words came out between breaths—"a woman with brown hair at Country Time. You'd better take along a couple of shots. You're going to need them." He staggered forward with a tray.

Ben went to grab another shot but Mike grabbed him. "Come on, let's go." When his boots hit the gravel, his friend chuckled and aimed them down the rough roadway. "That cougar was on the prowl for a younger man."

"You've been hanging out with Patrick too long," Ben muttered.

"Maybe. He was at Perkins the other day and tried to convince me that an eighty-year-old woman was a cougar and wanted him. You two need to get married—"

Ben gave his buddy a good-natured shove. "And let me guess. You and Laurie think you found just the gal."

Mike rubbed his arm and moved over a step. "There's no talking to you."

They continued in silence, wandering up and down the rows of trailers, RV's and tents. With no music playing on the stages tonight, everyone hung

41

out playing the typical drinking games like tippy cup or pong beer. Ben noted a number of campers appeared all played out, sitting and staring aimlessly into the campfires, listening to tunes from their cranked up radios.

The scent and sound of meat sizzling on grills had Ben's mouth watering. He could practically taste the juicy hot dog wedged in a pasty white bun. "Hungry?"

"Starved. Hey, I know just the place."

On the way to the food stand, Mike pointed out at least twenty women who matched Ben's description of Alex. Not one was even close. By the time he ordered a burger basket, he found he wasn't hungry. Thoughts of Alex actually being here had his stomach churning. He stood off to the side of the crowd, holding his untouched meal and watching Mike inhale his own food.

"If you're not going to eat that, I will." Mike tossed his empty tray into the garbage can.

Just then, a woman in the distance caught Ben's eye. The brim of the cowboy hat she wore shielded her face and he couldn't be sure. "Take it." He shoved the food at his friend and took off. He murmured apologies as he bumped and waded through the people. By the time he reached the spot, she was gone. He stood turning in a circle, scanning the sea of hats and heads.

"*Damn.*" Frustrated, he made his way back to the burger stand.

"Was it her?" Mike asked before popping the last of the hamburger into his mouth.

Ben shook his head and started walking.

Mike tapped his shoulder and pointed to a woman fifty yards away. "There's a woman in a tan hat."

"Not her," he managed to say, his tongue thick and dry. He reached for the package of gum from his shirt pocket. All he wanted was the hat back, and then he'd be over her for good.

At least he hoped so.

Ben shoved the stick into his mouth and offered the pack to Mike. "Want some?"

"Sure. Between the Jell-O and onions, I've a funky taste in my mouth."

It wasn't the taste of food or beverage that had Ben stuffing stick after stick of gum into his mouth. The tastes of cinnamon blazed through his mouth and he was hopeful. A minute later the flavor faded and the haunting taste of Alex's kisses were once again on the tip of his tongue. His shoulders slumped. *What kind of memory didn't fade with time?* He spit the useless gum out.

Absent-minded, he followed Mike away from the food area. When they arrived at the railroad tracks that bordered Hayfield, three security guards stood around checking for wristbands. People were free to wander to the different campgrounds as long as they had a wristband—four years ago, some drunk tried to take a shortcut to his campground by walking down the tracks late at night and was killed by a passing train. Ever since, security was tight, with signs and extra guards posted to make sure it didn't happen again.

They made their way down a path that eventually converged with the Gophers trail, which came from the east, and the Meadows trail that went to the south. All three trails merged at the cement underpass that crossed beneath the highway. This was the only way to the concert bowl and the four additional campgrounds. Police and security patrolled the highway and area, preventing pedestrians from foolishly crossing the busy highway itself.

The VIP campsite was one of the few campgrounds with available electricity. Huge rigs dwarfed the few tents staked out in the hard packed dirt. The place looked more like a retirement community for the rich than a weekend campground at a country music festival.

Mike pointed to a couple of pup-tents. "Probably for their kids?"

"Or their hired help." He waved a hand at the strings of lights hanging from rows of motor homes. The colorful lights draped over awnings and illuminating the tables and chairs that rested on green artificial turf. "Looks like Christmas."

Mike chuckled. "And on Sunday night it'll look like a ghost town."

A crowd stood a little further down the road next to a raised platform. Piled across the back of the stage was an elaborate set of karaoke speakers. Ben stopped next to an elderly couple. The man's plaid shorts, white shirt, socks and leather sandals paled in comparison to his companion's Dolly Parton hair, Tammy Faye make-up and four-inch heels. She swayed to the music, fingers flashing briefly with her brightly colored jewels as she settled her hand on her husband's forearm.

Mike poked Ben and pointed to a woman at the far edge.

"Nope."

He pointed to another, and Ben shook his head again.

"Your friend's a little picky," the older man next to Mike said.

"I'm not looking for just any woman, I'm looking for Alex. We met at Country Time last year."

The elderly woman's eyes lit up as her hands came to life, fluttering around. "How romantic! Wouldn't that be something if she was to walk up on the stage and they were reunited?" She tucked her hands around the man's waist as he bent to brush the platinum hair with a gentle kiss.

"Not exactly," Ben snipped. "Alex ran off with my autographed cowboy hat."

"No way." She gasped and slapped a jeweled hand to her cheek.

"Afraid so."

"Well, the little hussy shouldn't be able to get away with that."

"Now, now." The older man made shushing sounds. "Don't need to get riled over other's problems."

"We'll see about that." And, that said, she marched to the front of the stage.

Ben stood and watched in awe. He had no idea how the older woman didn't topple over on those thin heels.

"Excuse me," she said, coming to a halt in front of the microphone. "I know someone who needs our help." She pointed to Ben and everyone in the crowd turned his way. "Come on up and tell them what you told me."

What have I gotten myself into? Luckily, he'd had just enough to drink that he swaggered toward the stage, bumping into a very pretty blond on his way up. "Excuse me, miss."

She gave him the once over—more than once. He searched his pocket for his gum and slipped a stick into his mouth. There was a time when an appreciative glance from a pretty little gal would warm his blood. Now, the best he could do was pretend as he flashed a practiced smile. The gum instantly soured in his mouth.

He removed it, stepped next to the microphone and took a deep breath. "My name is Ben. Last year I was dancing here with a pretty woman. I thought she was a good-hearted one, but she turned out to be less than honest. We were getting along so good, set my autographed Toby Keith hat on her head, turned around...and both were gone. Her name is Alex and she has brown hair and is about this tall." He held his hand up once again to indicate her height.

Above the murmurs from the crowd, the Karaoke D.J. said, "Doesn't look like anyone knows her. Bummer about the hat. Can't say the same about the girl." He handed Ben a beer.

He drank down half. "Do you think I could send a song out?"

"No problem."

He thought for a moment and then asked, "Do you have Keith Urban's *You'll Think of Me?*"

The D.J. grinned. "Good choice." He turned, setting up the equipment.

As he did, Ben searched the crowd. If she wasn't here, maybe the words would drift over to her.

The instrumentals vibrated through the speakers and his body. A moment later the words appeared on the monitor, not that he needed them. The beat and rhythm flowed through him and he sang with his eyes closed. He knew the words by heart—the thought that someday she'd feel the pain of wanting him had been his constant companion this past year.

His voice was sure and strong as he started to adapt the words to his own pain...

"...*Ever since you found my autographed hat in your arms, I've been trying my best to get along. Hatless, I walked the streets alone with the sun beating down on me, but that's okay I got a nice tan. None of the gals seem to mind. When the sun kissed cowboy comes into town. So, take my hat. I don't need it. I'll never use it. But someday you'll think of me...you'll think of me.*"

The crowd cheered and Ben opened his eyes, watching as a brute of a guy walked up to the blond and put his arm around her. She winked at Ben.

His eyes slid shut, the memory of his arms around Alex once again fresh in his mind. "*Hey baby, why did you have to go and steal my hat and run away? I would have loved you when the sun went down. Whoaaaa whoooooooooooo, baby. Would have loved you when the sun went down, baby."*

Ben finished the song to a roar of approval from the audience. Smiling, he stepped off the stage.

A stranger slapped him on the back. "Hey buddy, sorry to hear about the woman. Wanna beer?"

"Thanks." He took the beer.

After a few more steps an older, slight man in a western shirt with pearl buttons and stiff denim jeans tapped his arm. "Women." He held up a can of beer, his face etched in pain. "Want one?"

"Might as well. Can't seem to live without either."

"Got that right." The man's leather face crinkled. "Hey D.J.," the man yelled out. "Got that song about faster women, older whiskey and more money?"

A laugh rolled through the crowd.

"How about *Cheatin' Heart?"* the D.J. answered back.

The bowed-legged cowboy pumped his arm. "Yes, sir." He handed Ben the can and started making his way up to the stage.

A sassy little brunette sidled up next to him. "Hope you find your hat."

He glanced down, saw the yellow wristband, and knew she was under twenty-one. "Me, too," he mumbled, nodding, not giving her a second glance.

"Come on." Mike tugged on Ben's arm. "We better go back or I might end up having to look for my wife."

"Yeah. With my luck, Julia might be kissing pirates by now."

They left the glow of the VIP campgrounds and headed toward the darkened underpass.

"It's really dark. What do you think? After ten?"

"I wonder how mad Laurie's going to be."

"Mad." Ben shouted over the blare of music as they finally entered their campgrounds. At two o'clock in the morning everyone had to shut their music off, but until then, it got louder the later it got.

It was impossible to carry on a conversation while walking down the road. Toby Keith's, *Should Have Been a Cowboy,* blared in full stereo from someone's radio. Ben smiled at thoughts of his younger brother, Dustin, dancing around the front yard and singing off key that one line over and over again...*Been a Cowboy...Been a Cowboy.* He'd gallop, laugh and sing to words and pictures only he could see. People had placed many labels on Dustin, special needs, Down's syndrome, retarded, but to Ben, he was just his little brother.

As they continued on, Ben kept thinking about how thrilled his younger brother, Dustin, would be if he could finally put that autographed hat on his head. There was only one thing Dustin liked better than being pushed in the oversized tire swing that hung from the huge oak tree on his parents' farm, and that was listening to Toby Keith.

The gravel crunched beneath his boots and he rubbed his arms; the friction warmed his skin, but did nothing for his bone-weary chill. "It's cold."

"Yeah, we should hurry. The thought of my wife sitting cold and lonely by the fire..."

Ben resisted the urge to gag and had to jog to keep up with his friend. At the fork in the road, his buddy started to the left. Ben shook his head, took two quick steps and grabbed his arm, pulling him to the right. "It's this way to the tent."

Mike stopped and turned slowly around. "Are you sure?"

"If you weren't daydreaming, you'd remember."

His smile turned sheepish. "Someday you'll understand. You'll fall hard for some gal and when you do..."

Ben gave him a shove. He'd already been down that road and knew how the song ended—the woman had walked into the sunset with his hat.

When I get the hat back, when I see her again, then *I'll be able to erase her from my thoughts.*

What was it about her? He had dated lots of pretty women, and he certainly didn't believe at love at first sight, so why wouldn't her memory leave him alone? His boots dragged through the gravel. Damn! The sooner that happened, the better.

Mike's steps quickened as the small glow of the campfire came into view. "Hey, honey," he called, his mouth split open in a big grin.

Laurie stood and rushed toward Mike's open arms. Ben shook his head as Julia stood up and staggered in a drunken strut toward him.

"Whoa." He rushed forward to steady her. "Let me guess, Jell-O shots?"

She giggled, and then swore. "That damn pirate. He was teaching me how to play Polish horse shoes and ladder golf. But it didn't seem to matter if I won or lost, I always had to take a sip of beer." Her hands clenched onto the front of his shirt.

Ben narrowed his eyes across the fire.

The corner of Patrick's mouth tugged up into a half smile. He shrugged. "How could I have known she was a lightweight? I don't think she had more than two or three beers."

"Good night." Laurie called out to the group in general before she disappeared into the tent with Mike.

Julia swayed to the right when she tried to wave and Ben scooped her up. "Come on. You'd better sit down before you fall down." He carried her over to one of the chairs around the campfire and set her in it. He ran a hand through his hair and eyed up the chair next to her. Suddenly the tension and disappointment from the day seemed too much to bear, and he dropped into the chair, suppressing a sigh as he stretched out his legs.

Julia wasted no time crawling out of her chair and onto his lap.

"Hold me, cowboy," she whimpered, laying her head on his chest.

His arms went around her automatically and a moment later he heard snoring from the redhead on his chest and giggling from Mike and Laurie's tent. *Just great.*

"Would you look at those three lovely wenches." Patrick leapt to his feet and started off after a group of women on the roadway. "Lovely ladies, wait up and let me do the honor of escorting you safely to your destination."

Ben chuckled, once again amazed at Patrick's never ending optimism.

His chest tightened as he stared at the fire. Even with a woman in his arms, he felt alone. He reached for the gum in his pocket, but Julia's head prevented him. She murmured and clutched his shirt tighter as he shifted her weight.

Weary, he gave up, closed his eyes and tipped his head back. Visions of a green-eyed woman danced behind his eyelids and tonight—maybe because she could be so near—instead of chasing thoughts of Alex away, he let the images remain.

If she hadn't fled, would she be the one in his arms tonight? Would it be her breath warm on his neck...and why couldn't he love the one he was with instead?

Julia's hand brushed against his cheek. "Hold me tighter, cowboy."

His grip tightened around her, but it wasn't her slight body his mind held.

Chapter Four

Alex couldn't help but feel discouraged as they walked back to their campsite. The campgrounds were larger than she remembered and there were so many more people. She didn't see anyone that looked like Ben and couldn't decide what would be worse, never running into him...or finding him with another woman. For a day that had started out as shiny and bright as a newly minted penny, the ending was a disappointment.

The steady presence of Shellie's arm came around her shoulder.

"Are you okay?"

"Sure."

Thankfully, Shellie's attention darted to their campsite and her friend began to shout. "Joe's here! And he brought chairs!"

Shellie might be fluttering her lashes at Joe and the fire, but Alex's gaze was fixed on the chairs. She couldn't believe they had forgotten to pack them.

"Hope you don't mind that I made a fire," he began. "And I couldn't find your chairs so I brought some over. That offer of a beer still good?"

Shellie opened up the cooler and pulled out a can. "Of course! Have a seat." She handed him a beer and pulled a chair close to his.

"Thanks for the seats, Joe." Alex grinned, plopped down into an empty chair and stretched her long legs out, flexing her heels and curling her toes. "We must have walked over twenty miles." She kicked off her sandals and cringed at her dirt encrusted toes. "No one would know I spent thirty-five dollars getting a pedicure."

"No one will care." Joe chuckled and stirred the fire with a stick. "Come Sunday everyone looks like dirt."

Alex raised a brow. "That makes me feel so much better."

"I didn't mean—"

"It's okay," Shellie interjected, patting his knee. "She's just tired and cranky."

"Yeah, I didn't mean anything."

She listened to their neighbor's radio for a while, Shellie and Joe's voices fading into the background as she let the music take her deep into her own thoughts.

The image of Ben suddenly blurred, and instead of herself, she saw his arm wrapped around another woman's waist. He tilted his head closer, she'd whisper, they'd laugh... Her veins turned to ice. It was the not knowing that was driving her crazy. She swallowed, but it was more than that. After the funeral, when her dad was still in the hospital, the only thing that kept her going was thinking of Ben and being reunited—he was going to be her silver lining, the one bright, shining hope amongst the darkness of their family's tragedy.

At the most random moments, his image would pop into her head. She could be under a car, wrenching on an oil filter, and she'd remember the gentleness in his touch, the way he squinted into the sun and the taste of his kisses.

The electricity of his memory melted the ice that had stopped her heart and a smile pulled at the corners of her mouth. Heat radiated throughout as she thought of how he'd wrap his arms around her when they met again. She was due for some luck and magic. He just had to be here.

She'd spent all year imagining she was

wrapping her hands around something other than wrenches and oil filters. At night, she wished her pillow was Ben's chest. He'd pull her tight and whisper it was okay when she woke up in the middle of the night from the same nightmare.

Your mother is gone. The words from last year still haunted her, echoing painfully through her heart.

"Hey."

She startled as a hand brushed her shoulder and Shellie's voice scattered her thoughts.

"She says yes, and she doesn't care," her friend called.

"Don't care about what?" Alex blinked and tried to bring the hypnotic flames into focus.

"What's on the pizza? What's the matter?" Her friend's eyes narrowed. "Haven't you been listening to anything I've said?"

Alex dropped back into the canvas chair, rubbing her arms in the suddenly cooled night air. The scent of burning logs hung in the air. "Sorry." She glanced around wondering if Joe thought she was drunk or crazy staring into the fire.

She sniffed. *Something smelled good.* She turned and saw Joe on the edge of the gravel road waving his hands.

Alex tried to shake the fog from her head. When she saw the pizza delivery truck, everything began to make sense. She inhaled again and her stomach rumbled. *Hot pizza, mmmm.*

The driver stopped next to Joe. Shellie passed out napkins and paper plates and, in seconds, he stood in front of Alex, lifting the white cardboard top off the box. Steam rose from the melted, gooey cheese as Joe offered her the first slice.

"Thanks. This is great." She licked her lips as the heat and grease soaked through the plate. Not waiting for it to cool, she bit into the piece. Alex couldn't even remember the last time she had eaten. Mmmmm. She smiled and nodded her approval to Joe.

He offered the next slice to Shellie.

"Ugh," she shouted as the piece slipped from the box and down her chest.

Alex's body vibrated with a suppressed laugh. When Joe sat down and bit into his own slice with gusto, a glob of pizza sauce dripped down his chin. She muffled a chuckle with her napkin. *Oh yeah, those two are made for each other.*

Another slice later, belly full, she tucked her legs up on her chair and settled back to listen to Joe's stories of Country Times past.

"So," he smirked, leaning forward in his chair, the fire casting shadows over his face. "This woman decides to go skinny dippin' in Lake Harriet. She was gone so long, her boyfriend thought she had drowned so they called for a helicopter and the water patrol." He paused, and then popped the last of his pizza in his mouth, continuing around the mouthful. "The woman was doing the backstroke across the lake without a stitch of clothing when the helicopter shone their spot lights on her. You wouldn't believe the number of guys that lined up along the edge of the water with binoculars on her."

Alex had no trouble picturing the men crowding the shoreline. "Guys! They're all the same when it comes to a women's naked body. They act like twelve year olds."

Joe laughed, and tossed the finished box into the fire. "I'd like to argue the point, but I'm out numbered."

Bone weary, Alex nodded. "Smart man."

She said her good nights and crawled into the tent figuring she'd give Shellie some time alone with Joe.

At least one of us is getting lucky this weekend.

****

Alex woke up the next morning with every bone in her body aching. Next year, she was bringing an air mattress.

She crawled out of the tent and blinked in the glare of the sun breaking through the trees. The air was heavy and still, the campgrounds quiet. The starlet came and stood next to her, looking anything but glamorous as she scratched her stomach and stretched.

"Do you know what time it is?" Alex asked.

The starlet yawned and checked her watch. "Nine. Wasn't that sweet of Joe? Chairs, fire and a pizza...he's so sweet. You wouldn't believe how much we have in common, too. It's like I've known him forever, and he's so easy to talk to..."

As Alex listened to the mooning ramblings, she smiled, lifted her damp hair off her neck and fanned herself by billowing air underneath her T-shirt. When Shellie stopped to take a breath, Alex added, "It's hot." Not because she wanted to change the subject, but at the moment that was all she could think of.

"It's the humidity that makes it seem so hot. You know what I could go for?" Shellie asked.

"A five star hotel with room service?"

The starlet's fingers tangled in her hair as she tried to brush it from her eyes. "I'd settle for a shower right now. Want to go?"

Alex nodded, looking down once again at her dirt-encrusted toes. "Ugh, it wasn't a nightmare—my feet really are that dirty. And it would be just my luck to run into Ben when I'm streaked with dirt. Let me grab a towel." She reached into the tent, pulled out her backpack and dug through it.

"We should put up a clothes line so we have someplace to hang our wet stuff." Shellie crawled around Alex and disappeared into the tent, tossing

55

out a length of rope. "I'll just be a minute while I gather up my things."

While she waited, Alex tied the line to the tent. There wasn't a tree close enough so she tied the other end to the back of a chair.

The *putt-putt-putt* of a golf cart drowned out the song of the birds in the overhead tree.

Shellie's head popped out of the tent like a contestant on a popular game show. "Hey! Joe!" Arms out and waving, she flew from the tent. Instantly, her feet tangled in the backpack and her face hit the dirt.

Alex ran to her side. "Are you okay?"

Within seconds, Joe was also there, helping Shellie to sit up.

Alex swallowed, her throat tightening at the sight of red blood staining her friends hair. She quickly grabbed a towel out of the offending backpack and began applied pressure to the wound.

"I'm bleeding?" Shellie's voice was just above a whisper. Her eyes grew wider as color drained from her face.

"It's only a small cut," Alex lied to keep her friend from panicking. Shellie had an aversion to the sight of blood, especially her own. "No big deal, but I don't have any Band-Aids."

Joe wrapped his arm around Shellie. "Come on. I'll take you to the first aid station, they've got plenty."

Shellie wobbled, ready to swoon. "I don't need stitches, do I?"

Alex pasted on a smile. "I've had paper cuts deeper than that. All you need is a bandage."

With one hand still holding the cloth firmly, she helped Joe get the wounded one into the golf cart, and then sat protectively on the other side.

Joe turned the key. "You know, you didn't have to go through all this trouble to get a ride in my cart.

All you had to do was ask."

"Now he tells me." Shellie grinned as they started bumping along down the path.

As the color crept back into her friend's complexion, Alex's shoulders relaxed.

"First aid is past the showers, close to where you came in," Joe offered. He continued to act like a tour guide, pointing out things and people he thought were interesting.

Her friend nodded and grinned. Joe continued a purposefully distracting commentary, endearing him to Alex.

Joe pointed to two white semi-trailers. "Showers."

Alex's chin dropped when she saw the number of people in line. By the time they got Shellie fixed up and back to the showers, the lineup would be astronomical.

Her shoulders slumped...then her heart stopped. *Oh my God! Ben.* She sat straight up, watching him walk down the steps from the semi-trailer showers' and wearing only khaki shorts and flip-flops.

"Stop!" Alex shouted, sliding to the edge of her seat as Joe put the brakes on.

Ben didn't even look up.

Shellie's head bobbed. "What?"

Alex tore her gaze from Ben, her stomach tightening at the sight of the blood-stained towel. Guilt pulled at her. It didn't seem fair. She had waited a year for this moment.

Shellie would understand and Joe would be with her.

She glanced back at Ben. Her heart raced as he started walking in their direction. She was ready to shout, *"Over here,"* when the towel slipped from her hand and her eyes were drawn back to her friend's blood-matted hair. Her stomach sank. There was really no choice.

"Can we go?" Joe asked.

She nodded while her eyes sent a silent plea to Ben. *Please look up.*

Her friend touched her arm. "Are you okay?"

The shakiness in Shellie's voice weighed heavy on her. "Yeah, sorry. The towel slipped," she offered lamely. "Let's get you checked out."

Ben, her heart cried out. Her limbs ached from restraint. Heart beating faster with each wish that he would just look in her direction, the only thing rooting her to the cart was her loyalty to her friend.

Alex's back stiffened and she swallowed a silent scream as he stopped to talk to a red-haired woman waiting in line.

"Are you sure you want me to go?" Joe asked.

She turned, applied more pressure to the towel and made eye contact with Joe. "Yeah, let's go." Her head swiveled back to find Ben as the last word came out.

A tiny, red-hot pain pricked the inside of her chest. He was only thirty feet away. She watched as a small drop of moisture slid down his defined chest, over his taunt abdomen and disappeared below the waistband hung low on his hips. If only he'd look up, she knew he'd see her.

He turned in her direction

The cart moved then so she couldn't be sure, but she thought their eyes had met for just a fraction of a second. Alex couldn't stop her heart from breaking. She wanted to cling to Ben like that droplet of water. To have her hands and mouth trail over his smooth, tan skin.

The cart picked up speed and soon Ben was out of sight. But not out of her thoughts. She had been *so close.* Tears of frustration stung her eyes. Did he see me? Recognize me? She tried to console herself with the concrete knowledge that he was here, but that did little to stop the teardrop that trailed down her cheek. With her free hand, she quickly brushed the evidence away, and applied more pressure to the wound with her other. Her stomach churned. After all Shellie had done for her this last year—helping her plan her mother's funeral, keeping her company in the hospital and listening to her talk non-stop about Ben—she couldn't believe she'd even thought of leaving her friend in this time of need.

The cart puttered to a stop beneath the white banner with a red cross painted on it. The closer they moved toward the large surplus tent, the paler Shellie got. A silver-haired nurse met them at the doorway. Alex blinked a number of times as her eyes adjusted to the lady's bright yellow pants and red, flowered smock.

She leaned Shellie up against Joe and stepped forward. In hushed tones, she quickly explained the situation and her friend's queasiness around blood. The nurse gave Alex a wink and instructed Joe to help the patient to a cot.

"We see it all the time," the nurse said in an understanding whisper.

Her smile put Alex's concerns at ease.

Quickly and efficiently, she examined the wound. "Cuts on the forehead always bleed more than anywhere else and they look much worse than they are." Efficiently, she dressed the wound and instructed Shellie to take it easy for the rest of the weekend.

After getting a reminder to apply sunscreen, they climbed back into the golf cart and started bouncing off down the road. Alex eagerly scanned the campsites on the way back to their tent. Her eyelids fluttered shut for a brief moment as she offered up a prayer. *Please let me find him again.* It would be so unfair if she left Country Time with only his hat and visions of his half-naked body to keep her company for another year.

The worst of it was, he didn't even know she was here looking for him, or why she left so suddenly last year. She wanted a chance to explain, to see him again. Her heart pounded as she resisted the urge to jump out of the slow moving cart and run through every single campsite asking if they knew Ben.

How could he be this close and she wasn't able to see him? An adrenaline rush had the hair on her arms standing straight up. *He had to be staying in Hayfield! Otherwise he wouldn't have been using* those *showers.*

If she had to walk through every campsite and talk to every person, there was no way she was going to leave without seeing him again.

Chapter Five

Joe stopped in front of their tent, shutting off the cart. He offered his arm to Shellie. "Let me help you."

"I'm fine." She held onto his arm anyway and rested her head on his shoulder. "You heard the nurse; it looks worse than it is."

"I also heard her say you needed to take it easy." He walked her over to a chair and sat her down. "Maybe you shouldn't be sitting. Maybe it would be better if you lay down."

Joe's radio crackled to life. He pulled the unit from its holster and held the device close to his ear. A moment later he transferred it to his mouth. "Had an emergency first aid run. I'll be right there," he spoke into the walkie-talkie before clipping it back into place.

"I'm fine." Shellie slouched in the chair and brushed a hand across her forehead. "I don't want you getting into trouble."

By his frown, it was evident Joe was having a tough time deciding as he paced between Shellie and the golf cart. He readjusted his baseball cap. "I don't feel right, just leaving you."

"Don't be silly. Alex is here and you can check up on me tonight." Her hopeful smile was all teeth.

Joe stopped beside her, bending to crouch at her level. "Are you sure?"

She reached out, pulled him close, and brushed his cheek with a kiss. "You're the sweetest."

He placed a matching kiss on her forehead. By

the time he stood up, Shellie's face had the soft, glowing appearance of a woman in love.

Alex was happy for her friend, but at the same time, she couldn't sit around the campfire all day when she knew Ben was out there. She needed to get moving and find him. "While you rest, I think I'll head on over to the showers."

Shellie sat upright. "You're not going without me."

Joe rested his hand on Shellie's shoulder. "I don't want you walking all that way and then standing in the sun. Across the railroad tracks at the VIP campgrounds they have a bath house. The shower lines are never very long. I can drive you over."

The muscles in Alex's neck throbbed. *But Ben isn't at the VIP campground; he's in Hayfield.*

"Maybe Joe is right and you should rest. I wouldn't be gone very long."

Shellie sat up straighter in her chair. "You're acting like *you're* the one that hit your head. Didn't you see how long the lines were at the showers? You'd be there all day."

She swallowed. "It'd be nice to get a little exercise before my shower. Maybe I'll go for a quick run and then, if you're feeling better, we can go over to the VIP area."

Joe's radio crackled again. "What's it going to be ladies?"

Shellie shook her head. "You've never ran a day in your life." Her arms folded across her chest. "You're acting weird. If you want me to stay, it's okay—just say so."

Guilt dropped her stomach to her knees. "Of course I want to go with you. Just a minute, Joe, let me get our things." Taking a deep breath, she kept telling herself, *everything's going to work out.*

Alex ran back into the tent for their necessities

and the hat. She climbed back into the golf cart and gasped at her dust covered legs. "Thanks, Joe, for offering us a ride. I can't wait to wash away five pounds of dirt."

"Thanks, Joe," the starlet repeated breathlessly. Her hand rested on his arm, her glow clearly visible through her grime-streaked face.

With the hat on her lap, Alex pulled her sweaty, dusty hair up into a pony tail. She placed the hat on top to hide the mess. Her hand lingered on the brim. Maybe it would be better if she didn't run into Ben until *after* she had her shower. If she were to kiss him now, they'd only make mud. The thought had her chuckling at her own humor.

Shellie poked her. "Are you sure you're okay?"

"I am now."

They were less than a block away from the railroad crossing when Joe's walkie-talkie began to crackle again. He pulled to the side of the gravel road and listened to the broken voices.

"Looks like I've got to get back to the entrance. Do you think you can walk from here?"

"No problem for me." Alex stepped out of the cart and grabbed her bag. "I don't know about Shellie."

Joe's hand captured Shellie's arm. "I'm sorry, if you can't. I'll bring you up to the front and—"

"Don't be silly. I'm fine. Besides, Alex can carry my stuff." Shellie leaned in, placing a loud, smacking kiss on his lips. "You're the best."

Alex's mouth split into a grin as Joe blushed. She reached into the cart and hefted the injured starlet's bag. "Thanks again."

He nodded, but never took his eyes off Shellie. Alex watched his Adam's apple bob. *He has it bad.*

With one last wave, they turned toward the railroad tracks. "Ouch!" Alex yelped as something hit her backside. She jumped around. Golf balls on a string appeared to be laughing at her from the ground.

A man jogged toward her. "I'm sorry. My friend's a terrible shot."

"What are they?" She bent down, picked up the golf balls and handed them back to the bare-chested man wearing a yellow bandana.

Shellie rolled her eyes. "Ladder golf."

"Oh yeah, ladder golf. I'm certain I saw it on ESPN or was it the Olympics?" Alex readjusted the bags on her shoulder. Her friend could certainly be a know-it-all.

Shellie smirked at the man. "My friend doesn't get out much."

"I get out plenty," Alex defended herself. She moved Shellie's bag to her other shoulder, uncertain what was in there, but it sure was heavy. "I've just never camped before. Unlike someone else I know, I wasn't a Girl Scout."

"We have something in common," the bandana man said. "I like eating Girl Scout's..." He paused, his eyes twinkled and the last word came out soft and low. "Cookies."

Alex's insides turned to jelly. Something about the way he said cookies and slid his tongue across his upper lip lightened her mood.

"You know, it's not safe for beautiful women like yourselves to be out wandering alone." This time his tongue traced his bottom lip. "I would be willing to offer you my services..."

Shellie laughed. "I think what we may need is protection from *you*. If I was Little Red Riding Hood I'd be worried about my grandma right now."

"What?" Alex and the bandana man asked in unison.

A small crowd had gathered, presumably the others who had been playing ladder golf.

Shellie let out an exasperated breath. "He's a

pirate—"

"So?" Alex interrupted. *Okay, yeah. He does look like a pirate.* She shook her head and pointed to the Band-Aid on her friend's head. "She bumped her head," she offered as an excuse then turned back to Shellie. "The only people in Little Red Riding Hood are the girl, the wolf, Grandma, and the woodsman."

"I *know* that," the starlet dramatized in a big drawl. "But the way he keeps licking his lips makes me think he'd like to be the wolf and eat grandma."

A collective laugh sprung from the group. Shock replaced the puzzled look on Shellie's face and her eyes became huge. She clamped her hands over her mouth, mumbling, "I didn't mean eating *that* way."

There was a slight pause and then belly laughs erupted from the crowd. Thankfully, Shellie joined in the chorus of laughter this time.

With the fading of the laughter came an invite to play tippy cup from a clean-cut guy in navy shorts and a white polo.

Alex hiked the bags higher onto her shoulder. "Sorry, got to go."

"Just one game?" The pirate stepped closer. His smile faded to a slow sexy pout. "Please."

"I don't know." Alex shrugged. "We were on our way to the showers."

"If you wait a half hour the lines will be shorter," the bandana man coerced, tugging the whiskers on his chin while his gold earring glittered in the sun.

"Stay," the other men chimed in.

Shellie nodded her agreement and pointed to a chair in the shade. "Go ahead. I'll be sitting right over there."

Alex eyed up the other players as she followed Shellie. She wanted to play, she wanted to have fun, but she also wanted to find Ben. *One game.* She set the bags down next to Shellie. "Are you sure?"

"Go on," Shellie said. "I'll watch."

"But I've never played."

"It's easy." The pirate grabbed her hand and pulled her over to his side of the table. He set the plastic cup upside down with the rim hanging over the side of the table. With one finger, he tipped the cup upright. "It's that simple. When everyone on our team gets their cups upright, we win."

Two of the men on the other side of the table wore jeans slung low on their waist, their abs peaking out beneath their T-shirts. A third guy had on a muscle shirt and flexed his arm. The fourth fellow had been the one that had issued the invite.

On her side of the table was the pirate, a bald man covered in tattoos and the last teammate, all dressed in black. "Sure," she said, taking her place at the table. These men were no different than the guys who came into the garage. "Why not?"

The pirate poured what was left from his can of beer into her cup. She held up the plastic glass, staring at the amber liquid. "Isn't it a little early for beer?"

"It's five o'clock somewhere," the tattoo man shouted.

"And the breakfast of champions." The pirate's voice was warm on her ear.

She set the cup down. A smile parted her lips as she recalled her dad's advice to go a little wild this weekend. "What the heck." She nudged the pirate. "You only live once."

"That's the spirit, matey."

"Go," someone shouted.

She quickly drained her beer, and on the second try, tipped her cup upright. Shellie gave her the thumbs up sign.

"Come on." Alex shouted in encouragement to their man in black. "You can do it." Sure enough he did and a cheer went up.

With her hips shaking, she danced down the line, giving her teammates high fives before making her way back to the pirate, dancing a step or two with him. "That was fun. Thanks for the game."

He reached for her hand, spun her into his arms and continued the dance. "Hey, you can't go. We won. You have to stay until we lose."

Alex stopped moving and glanced across the table at a new group of four. Breathless, she turned back to her dance partner and whispered, "But I'm not much of a drinker."

He winked. "Don't worry. I won't let you get drunk." With a flip of his wrist and some fast footwork, he had her spinning out of his arms and released her hand. "By the way, my name's Patrick. Next to me is Red and on the end is Beau."

She glanced down the line giving each of them a smile as the guys nodded their greeting.

"I'm Alex. Nice to meet all of you." She grinned and gave Patrick a hip check. "You guys are a lot of fun."

"Alex." His finger reached out and touched the brim of her hat. "The hat looks warm. If you want, I'll go set it over there." He pointed to a lawn chair.

Her spine tightened. *Did he notice Toby's signature? Maybe he really was a wolf in pirate's clothing.*

She shook her head and took a step backward. No one touched the hat. "No thanks. My hair's a mess."

Patrick reached for his bandana. "I could trade you."

"Do you guys all know each other?" she interjected quickly, shaking her head and purposely changing the subject.

Patrick's smile took up most of his face. "I didn't mean to upset you." He placed his hands up in front of his chest. "I promise I won't touch your hat again."

67

Her gaze slid to the ground, she hadn't meant to be harsh. She softened her tone as she raised her eyes. "It's just that the hat has sentimental value."

"That's cool. And yes, for the most part, I know these guys." Patrick's hands once again settled casually down by his side. "Some of us play ball together. What about you—who's your friend?"

"That's Shellie." She pointed in the starlet's direction.

"Hey, Shellie," Patrick called out. "Do you mind waiting a little bit longer?"

The starlet gave her best Hollywood smile and waved her agreement.

"Great." Patrick reached for Alex's cup again, filling it a quarter full.

Alex's fingers poised on the edge of the cup. "Okay."

Less than a minute later, her team won again and she danced down the line giving high fives to her teammates before sashaying back to her spot.

The pirate reached out and traced the heart on her bicep. "You've got quite an arm on you."

Their eyes met. He pushed up the sleeve of his T-shirt, revealing a cross with *Father* written in script. There was no need for words in the bond forged through pain.

"Fill them up," Beau called out.

Patrick nodded silently, and turned her cup upside down. "Alex is done." He tipped his own cup over. "Hey, Dan and Rick! Come take our places."

Her spirits sagged along with the corners of her mouth. Her mom would have liked Patrick. She could almost hear her innocently asking, *"Where did you get the earring?"* The thought warmed her like most of her memories of her mother.

She waved to the guys standing at the table then tilted her head and smiled to bandana man. "Thanks for the game, Patrick. It was nice meeting you."

He draped his arm around her shoulder. "I told you I wouldn't let you get drunk." He gave her a half hug. "It's been three years for me."

She didn't need to ask, she knew he was talking about his loss. "Barely a year." she replied, her voice no louder than a whisper.

"I'm sorry."

"Thanks." She gave him a hug, soaking in his strength and compassion. "Me, too."

When he stepped back, his hands slid down her arms and captured hers. "Come on then." He dropped one of her hands and walked her back to the spot where Shellie sat. "Got a pen and a piece of paper?" he asked.

"I do!" The grinning starlet shouted, searching through her backpack. "Here it is."

Alex's eyes widened. "No wonder that bag is so heavy." She chuckled. "Why would anyone bring paper and a pen to the shower?"

Her friend rolled her eyes. "Duh. For times like these when handsome men want to give us their number," she all but mouthed to Alex.

"Thanks." Patrick jotted a quick note. He handed the pen back to Shellie and the paper to Alex. "Promise me, if things don't work out you'll call me."

Her eyes narrowed as she studied the signature beside the phone number. "What things?" She glanced up to meet his steady gaze.

His hands gripped her shoulders. "Just promise."

She didn't know what he meant or even what she should say. But his tone compelled her to nod her agreement.

He gave a gentle squeeze. "Call me if things don't work out, okay?"

Again she nodded, not quite certain what she

was agreeing to.

Before she had time to dwell on it more, Shellie stood up. Alex hiked both bags up onto her shoulder. The starlet waved and shouted out good byes and they started down the dirt road.

They were almost to the campground border when they heard the deep whistles and saw the slow moving train in the distance. "If we run, I'm sure we can make it," Shellie said.

"Have you forgotten you've already had one accident today? And I'm not sure you should be running."

"Nonsense, I'll be fine." The starlet brushed the hair from her eyes and began to sprint.

"Then I don't think I should be running," Alex called after her, staggering to keep her balance beneath the shifting weight of Shellie's bag. "After all, I'm carrying the bag with the complete set of encyclopedias."

Shellie turned half way around, motioning with her arm. "Faster, *faster*."

She caught up to her friend as the warning lights began to flash. They hustled to the other side just as the crossing arms lowered into place.

"Just made it," Shellie panted.

Alex stopped, resting her hands on her knees. Her heart pounded and her lungs burned. She jerked around. "Did you hear that? Someone called my name." *Ben?* She moved closer to the crossing.

A strong hand clamped on to her forearm. "Move along now."

"You don't understand." She flashed the security guard her best smile. "Someone called my name and I just—"

The guard yanked her arm. "Now!"

"I just want to—"

Shellie gripped her free arm.

"Come on." She leaned close and whispered,

70

"You're making a scene."

After dragging Alex a couple of steps, the guard released his grip with a grunt. "Wait there." He pointed to an area where people grouped.

"What's gotten into you?" her friend asked as she continued dragging her.

"You can let go of my arm." Even though she grumbled at Shellie, she kept her eyes on the crowd. "My back will be bruised from your pack and my arm from your fingers," Alex accused, frustrated at the manhandling and being taken away before she had a chance to see who had called her.

Shellie released her grip. "Sorry."

"I know I heard someone call my name from the other side of the tracks." Alex relaxed her shoulders.

"Should we wait?"

When she turned to her friend, beads of sweat were visible on Shellie's forehead and nose. Her complexion had gone from rosy to pasty-white. Alex frowned, "Hang in there, okay. We're practically to the showers."

"Sure?"

She's a saint. "Of course I'm sure." With one last look back, Alex returned her focus where it should be, on her friend. "Let's go."

"I can't decide what has the greatest appeal, the shower or the flush toilets."

Alex glanced at her feet. "All I know is that camping makes you appreciate the finer things in life—like feet dusted with dirt instead of caked in grime."

Shellie's facial features softened and her eyelids drooped. "Like Joe."

She nodded. "Yeah, he's pretty cool."

Her friend's chest puffed out, her tongue clicked and some color came back to her cheeks. "He's more than pretty cool, he's great, funny, charming, thoughtful and cute—"

Chuckling, Alex gently nudged her. "A little sensitive?"

A crooked grin appeared then faltered. "Oh no! I've fallen for Joe."

"Yep, it certainly looks that way." Relieved to see the color in her friend's face and the sparkle in her eyes, Alex joined the line as it slowly moved in the direction of the showers.

In the interim wait, Alex couldn't help but wonder if it had been Ben's voice she had heard. If it was, then he'd seen her and he'd been searching for her. Her heart beat faster. If it hadn't been him...her smile faded and she willed the thought away.

They shuffled forward up the cement ramp to the entrance of the facilities. Inside the doorway, she paused as her eyes adjusted to the dim surroundings. To her right were eight stalls partitioned off with weathered grey walls and a variety of pastel-colored shower curtains. To the left was the shower area, which looked exactly like the toilet area except for the water on the floor and the bench and hooks outside the shower stalls.

As Alex waited in the silent shower line, she daydreamed about her reunion scene with Ben. His face would light up when their eyes met. He'd rush forward with open arms. He'd tell her how much he missed her, how worried he had been. Her lips tingled at the thought of his kisses.

Nudged from the side, Alex glanced over.

Shellie pointed. "There's an open shower. Oh, another one, come on, let's go."

Alex followed, tossing her stuff onto an open bench. Like high school gym class, she stripped down before entering the stall. The lukewarm water trickle over her skin, and—also like high school—a moment later, while her head was full of lather, the water turned cold. Even thoughts of Ben couldn't keep her warm. Hopping up and down beneath the spray, she got the last of the soap off and quickly shut of the water.

As she toweled off, she tried not to notice the naked woman next to her. Hard, with the colorful tattoos glaring on the pale skin. One leg held various tones of green that partially concealed a crouching tiger while the other leg looked like something from Jack and the Bean Stalk. Across her back was Pegasus and Alex diverted her gaze before figuring out what was what was tattooed around the woman's navel or splattered between her breasts.

"Do you like them?" the tattooed woman asked.

Alex nodded, too embarrassed to speak. She slid her clothes on her still damp body and hustled out the door. She followed the cement sidewalk around the corner to the backside of the women's bathroom where mirrors and outlets had been installed on the outside wall.

She spotted Shellie and moved in besides her. To find enough room on the shelf for Ben's cowboy hat she had to slide her friend's bottles, pencils, tubes and jars across the wooden plank

"I can see those years of Girl Scouts paid off. You really do come prepared. The only thing I remembered was shampoo and clean underwear." She pointed to a tube. "What's that?"

Shellie arched her eyebrow in a 'd'uh' motion. "Lip plumper."

Alex picked up the tube, slid the top off and studied the bright red crayon. "This is supposed to make your lips fat?" She cocked a doubtful brow and snapped the cap back on.

"Not fat. Full and pouty."

"Where did you get all this stuff?" She picked up a pencil with a built in sharpener.

"Karen's Kurls."

"Still taxiing the seniors to their hair appointments?"

"Tuesday and Thursday nights—endless brownies, coffee and gossip. Besides, the women buy all these products and when they don't work for them, they give them to me."

"An eighty-year-old wanted fat lips?" She laughed and ran the towel through her hair one last time.

"Actually, Nora is only sixty-seven."

Alex pointed to an aerosol can. "Let me guess, fat hair?"

"Just because you've never had a bad hair day doesn't mean that others haven't," Shellie muttered.

"No one would ever know. My hair is always tucked under a cap, beneath a bandana or in a ponytail."

Shellie's mouth popped open as she lined her eyelids.

Alex grabbed the hair dryer. "But no more cover-ups for me. Bring on the bad hair days."

She bent from the waist, tipped forward and aimed the hot air on her roots. While her fingers worked to remove the tangles, a pair of high-heeled sandals stopped within her vision.

When the shoes didn't move, she stood up and shut off the blower. She towered over a red-haired woman in matching red sandals.

The woman's lips pursed. Her hands rested on her hips and her elbows jutted out.

Alex pushed her bag closer to Shellie and moved Ben's hat atop it.

The woman's hand flew from her hip and she jabbed a well-manicured nail into Alex's collar bone.

"Ow!" She clenched her hands. "What's your problem, lady?"

Suddenly, it was so quiet Alex was certain she could have heard a Q-tip fall. With an eye on her opponent, she quickly assessed the situation. Almost everyone's mouths were as round as their eyes and she could almost hear the undertone, "*Fight, fight, fight.*"

Shellie stepped up to the woman, nose to nose. "Back off, Red."

Alex pulled the brave starlet back and stepped protectively in front of her friend.

"I'm only going to tell you this once," the redhead screeched in a loud, high-pitched voice. "Keep the hell away from my man!"

Chapter Six

"Are you talking about Joe?" Shellie's voice shook.

Alex blocked her friend from advancing. She wasn't concerned about her safety, but the other woman's—Shellie could be meaner than a junkyard dog and the tiny little redhead would be no match. Alex locked her knees and cringed when she felt the tips of her friend's fingernails dig into her shoulders, but she didn't budge.

The woman tossed her head from side to side and shouted, "No, I'm not talking about a Joe." She pointed her finger and poked the air at Alex. "You know damn well who I'm talking about and you better stay the hell the way."

She did an about face, her heels beating out an erratic tempo. Alex stood dumbfound as the angry chick exited across the cement sidewalk.

Shellie's grip loosened. "What is she talking about?"

She rubbed her shoulder and wished everyone would quit staring at her. They all couldn't seriously think she and Shellie were men stealers? The redhead was beautiful, petite and could run around in high heels. What man would choose a tomboy in a dress over someone as pretty as that?

She turned toward Shellie and whispered, "She obviously has me mixed up with someone else. Or maybe she's Patrick's girlfriend or wife?"

"The pirate?"

Alex shrugged. "Maybe. He's the only guy I've

talked to besides Joe."

Shellie let out a long, slow breath as her right hand fluttered across her chest. "I'm glad that crazy woman wasn't Joe's girlfriend."

She patted her friend's forearm. "I don't think you have to worry about Joe. He doesn't look like the cheating type."

With the last of her words still hanging in the air, she switched on the hairdryer and ignored the leftover onlookers. By the time the blower motor hummed off, her hair was dry and everything was back to normal. A group of teenage girls slid in next to them with an assortment of electric irons and straighteners.

Shellie's heart-shaped face glowed beneath the white bandage as she gathered up her beauty paraphernalia. Alex grinned and wondered if it was the make-up, the sun or thoughts of her new leading man. "You look good in love."

Shellie gave her a light shove. "Real funny."

As they retraced their steps to their campsite, Alex kept her eyes opened for the redhead, Patrick...and especially Ben. The first one she hoped she wouldn't run into again. The second was all right, but thoughts of bumping into Ben had her heart soaring as she replayed the scenario of his arms wrapped tightly around her. He just had to want her. True, she didn't have a lot of experience with boyfriends, but she was certain that look in his eyes was more than casual interest. Besides, he had given her his autographed hat—that had to mean something.

The pack weighed heavily on her shoulders and her thoughts weighed heavy in her heart. *Where was he?*

Shellie staggered into camp and plopped down in the first canvas chair she came to. "I'm so tired."

Alex searched the road one last time, before

walking over to her friend. She dropped Shellie's bag to the ground with a satisfying *thud*. "You should've tried carrying your backpack. I swear you have bricks in there."

"Just two of them." Her friend's arms stretched above her head as she yawned. "Before you sit down, would you mind getting me something to drink?"

"No problem." Alex opened the cooler and peered inside. "What's your pleasure...soda, beer or something for poison ivy?"

"Diet and maybe a granola bar."

Alex grabbed two of each and dropped into the adjacent canvas chair. She stretched her legs out, kicked off her sandals, and tried to quiet the butterflies in her stomach. *Just a matter of time now before I'm once again in Ben's arms.*

She bit into the granola, but had a hard time swallowing as images of the redhead woman flashed like a warning beacon in her mind. Alex put the half-eaten bar on the arm of her chair and reached into her pocket to pull out the slip of paper with Patrick's number on it. "Why would a man with a girlfriend or a wife give me his number? Let alone ask me to call if things didn't work out?"

Shellie pulled her mirrored sunglasses out of her bag. "I was wondering the same thing. Maybe he's a victim of spousal abuse and if you find him dead along the road you should call. Maybe it isn't his number he gave you, but the local police or maybe it's the number to a mortician."

"Yuk." The paper slipped from Alex's hand.

Hollywood leaned over, picked it up and handed it back. "We don't litter."

"Yes, ma'am." Alex slid the number back into her pocket and stood. Sometimes Shellie acted more like her neighbor, Mrs. Henderson.

She hung up the wet towels and tossed her bag next to the tent while listening to the music drifting on the breeze from the concert bowl. The sound system was set up so campers could hear everything that was going on up on the stage. Alex let the music fill her like a giant breath of air. When the song ended, an emcee talked about today's line-up, then the music was back on.

Shellie stood up and danced. "I wonder if Joe likes to dance." Sweeping a stick into her arms, she swayed and twirled. "I like to dance."

"Me, too." Alex stood and her feet glided over the ground. "I'll never forget dancing with Ben." She closed her eyes and her pulse quickened as she relived the moment. Her eyelids fluttered open. "I felt like Cinderella at the ball, when the prince sweeps her into his arms." She twirled until she reached her backpack, breathless and glowing. She dropped to her knees. If she had a say in anything, tonight would find her once again in Ben's arms. *The grease monkey whisked away by the handsome cowboy.* She giggled at the idea.

"Have you decided what you're going to wear tonight?" Alex let the material of her satin bra slide through her fingers as she dug through her belongings. She wanted to look hot and sexy for Ben. Could she actually pull off the look? There couldn't be a doubt in his mind when he actually saw her— one glance and all he'd want to do was whisk her away. But what if he took one look and laughed over the ridiculousness of him falling for someone as unexciting as her.

In one hand she held jeans, in the other a skirt. She shrugged and looked to Shellie for help. "What do you think? I'm worried if I wear the skirt I'll get cold when the sun goes down."

"It's only three o'clock. The sun won't set until after eight. Put on the skirt," Shellie replied confidently.

Alex twisted her lips. "Are you sure?"

"Yes. If you match it with a tank top, you'll be sexy, daring and, best yet, hard to resist."

"Okay." Alex kicked up her heels and disappeared into the tent. Thoughts of his large, tan hands spanning her waist tickled her thoughts as she peeled off her clothes. She grabbed a bottle of lotion, wanting to feel nothing like a tomboy; she'd rather be smooth to his touch. The fragrant lotion rushed from the bottle and pooled on her thigh. *I'll either be really soft or as slippery as a greased pig.* She massaged the moisturizer into her leg and worked her way down to her calf. "Ugh!" She hollered out when she got to her ankles. "Gross. My feet are still filthy."

"It's from the gravel roads," Shellie called back.

"Great, my hands are full of lotion, I'm in the middle of getting dressed and I'm starting to make mud." Alex searched for a clean spot on her body to smear the cream. Maybe this was a sign that this was all a hopeless gamble.

"Don't be so dramatic. Give me a minute." Her voice was all business. The starlet had clearly changed back into Girl Scout role. A moment later the flap from the tent opened and a box of baby wipes were tossed in. "Good thing one of us comes prepared." Shellie zipped the flap on the tent closed behind her.

"La-di-dah." Alex grabbed for the plastic box.

"You're a little cranky."

"Yeah, I am. I'm not even sure what I'm doing here. What if I shouldn't even be looking for Ben?"

Shellie dropped to her knees. "Sure you should. You're just nervous."

Alex shook her head. "More than nervous." She licked her lips. "Scared."

Girl-scout mode gone, the starlet smiled brightly. "A day ago, I wouldn't know what you were talking about, but after meeting Joe, I know that

80

feeling. When I'm with him I can't help but think that he is 'The One'. I imagine us back here next year, maybe spending Christmas together and then I think, 'Whoa, moving too fast,' then my stomach drops and I think, what if he doesn't like me, what if—" Shellie tossed her arms up. "Crazy, isn't it?"

Alex nodded. "Yeah, it is." She pulled a wipe from the box. "Thanks."

Shellie stood up. "I'll be in a chair if you need me." The zip of the tent closing followed her exit.

She had to put some muscle behind the baby wipes to get the dirt from the bottom of her feet. By the time she was done, the tent smelled like baby powder. Alex unzipped the door and tossed the wipes back outside. "Next time, buy unscented."

"What's wrong with smelling like a baby?"

Alex didn't bother to reply as she tugged on her raw-edge-frayed, faded denim skirt. Her hand rested on her stomach as she tried to settle the roller coaster feeling that persisted; one moment her heart was in her throat and a minute later it would land hard at the bottom of her belly. *Just nerves.* She pulled on a little white ribbed tank top. The shirt stretched over her chest and hugged her abdomen. She smoothed the material into place and tugged on the bottom of the skirt while the other hand pulled on the bottom of the shirt.

With her head bent at odd angles she checked for unintentional exposed body parts. *Maybe not.* With a ragged breath she reached for her backpack and checked out her options. *Crap!* Her palm tapped her forehead. *I should have just packed sweatpants.*

With a last look, she backed out of the tent, slowly stood and once again surveyed her outfit. The skirt hung low on her hips and the shirt ended right above her belly button ring. *Not bad.* Definitely the most skin she had exposed in a long time, but then that wasn't too hard to do when you spent your days wearing overalls.

"What do you think?"

Shellie's legs were propped over a chair. Her feet kicked the air as she slapped a hand to her stomach. "When did you get your navel pierced? Did it hurt?"

"Nope. Neither did the tattoo." She traced the heart on her arm, finding comfort in the act.

"Maybe I should get one."

"You realize tattoos and piercing both require needles."

"Eww, no way. I don't like needles." She shot up in her chair. "Hey, toss me my shoes. I don't want to get my feet dirty walking to the tent."

Alex picked up the shoes, but paused and decided against tossing them over—with Shellie's luck, she'd probably end up with a black eye.

After securing her shoes, Shellie disappeared into the tent. Alex tidied up and tried to keep her thoughts from focusing on Ben. Her palms ran over her skirt. When her friend reappeared she was wearing denim shorts and a red T-shirt with 'Red Neck Girl' splashed across her chest. Shellie raised her hands above her head and jumped up and down.

"Will you check to make sure my tummy doesn't show?"

Alex's hands rested on her hips as, with an indulgent smile, she watched the show. "Nope. No tummy showing."

"How about now?" Shellie continued moving to a tune that only she could hear. When her hands stretched high above her head again, she mouthed and spelt out Y-M-C-A with her arms.

Alex joined in, dancing and singing along until they collapsed in their chairs in a fit of giggles. The stress and tension that had settled in her neck lessened with each whoosh of laughter. When she had caught her breath and brushed a tear from her eye, she stood and walked over to the Mustang to check her reflection in the side mirror.

"Don't bother looking. You're gorgeous. Not a hair out of place."

"Thanks." She turned around. "You, too. And don't worry, there is nothing immodest about you. The Girl Scouts would still be proud to claim you as one of their own."

Shellie batted her eyelashes and ruffled her hair with her fingertips. "And Joe?"

"He'd be a fool not to claim you."

Her eyes were wide and hopeful. "You think so?"

Alex nodded. "For sure. Come on, let's hit the road."

"Let me grab a couple bottles of water...and don't forget Ben's hat."

"On it."

"And my sunglasses."

"Sure thing." Alex set the hat on her head and exchanged Shellie's glasses for a bottle of water.

Hollywood cleaned her shades with the edge of her shirt. "Two nights left. Do you think he's even here?"

With her friend's glasses askew, they headed down the dirt path. Alex sipped on her water.

Shellie's finger brushed her arm. "Well?"

She hesitated then whispered, "What if I said I already saw him?"

Shellie latched on to her arm, and like an anchor, brought them to a halt. "What? When?"

Alex broke the death grip to move out of finger-poking range. "As we drove by the showers on the way to the first aid station. He was walking down the steps." As her body heated up, she fanned herself with Ben's cowboy hat. "I'm telling you, Shellie, my memory didn't do him justice. And without a shirt...wow, you wouldn't believe the chest on—"

Mirrored sunglasses perilously close to falling off, Shellie jumped in front of her and clasped her shoulders. "You should have said something. Why didn't you tell me? How can I help if I know nothing?"

Alex stepped back. "You're crushing his hat." She placed the Stetson on her head for safekeeping, wrapped an arm around her friend's jittering shoulders and turned her back toward the road. "Come on. It's not a big deal. I'll run into him again." Cautiously she started down the path. "I have to."

Hollywood pushed her glasses back up and fell into step. "It *is* a big deal. *Huge.*"

Her steps slowed as her emotions crested in her tummy. "I should have told you." A shiver stole up her spine. "What if he doesn't want me? What if he's found someone else?"

"It'll work out."

"What if every time he holds me all I can remember is the tragic phone call? Or what if I look at his face and only want to cry with the sorrow of my mom's passing, what then?"

Shellie's smile softened. "You're just borrowing trouble thinking that way."

Alex's thoughts were spinning so fast, she was dizzy. The path tilted with a horrible realization and she stopped cold.

Twenty feet later, her friend did the same and spun around. "What?" she asked, returning to her side.

"Oh my God! That woman—the redhead from the shower. I know where I saw her before." Alex clutched her friend for support. "She was at the other showers we drove by this morning. I'm certain she's the same chick Ben stopped and talked to." Letting go of her friend she doubled her arms around her stomach. "I think I'm gonna be sick."

"Stop this. You don't know for sure. There are a lot of redheaded women here that could fit that description."

Everything hurt.

"Hey, darlings, come and get a Jell-O shot," a deep baritone voice called out.

"See." Shellie pointed to a crowded campsite.

Alex glanced in the direction of her friend's finger. She caught a glimpse of a redheaded woman in a black bikini top and low-slung black shorts holding a silver tray with red Jell-O squares that bounced and jiggled like jolly Saint Nick's belly.

She shrugged, walked over and accepted a tiny plastic cup and held up the shot. "Thank you." After letting the fruity square slide down her throat, Alex crushed the container and tossed it in the garbage.

A dark-haired man with an unsteady gait and a number twenty-three Vikings jersey approached. "Nice hat." Trailing right behind him was a guy in an orange T-shirt advertising Dave's Bar and Grill.

Alex smiled sweetly and stepped back.

"Is that hat autographed?"

The orange-shirted dude moved closer and she could see the stains marring the front of his clothes. Hesitantly, she nodded and slid back another step.

He poked number twenty-three in the ribs. "The guy that was here last night lost an autographed hat. Think there's a reward?" His voice cackled as he exposed yellowed teeth.

An older woman in a navy skirt and white sweater stepped next to the men. Alex breathed a sigh of relief. *Probably someone's mother and surely a voice of reason.*

"You got it wrong." The older woman stated as she moved closer to Alex. "The hunky cowboy that was here last night didn't *lose* his hat; it was stolen by some crazy woman right off the top of his head."

Alex's heart hammered against her rib cage. A hand clamped onto her arm and her knees went weak.

"Let's get out of here." Shellie tugged hard on

her arm. "Come on."

Her voice was insistent and Alex stumbled as her friend dragged her backward toward the road.

"Hey," number twenty-three called.

Shellie spun Alex around. "Run!"

Chapter Seven

Their feet pounded the dirt-packed road as they ran toward the railroad tracks. Their pace didn't slow until the crossing arms came into view. Alex glanced over her shoulder. Seeing no one, she stopped, tipped over at the waist and gasped for air. The hat tumbled from her head.

She picked it up, resisting the urge to send the Stetson sailing down the empty tracks. "I can't believe he's telling strangers I'm a thief!"

"You"—Shellie sucked in a gasp of air—"don't know that." Her chest heaved as she moved to the edge of the trail.

Alex crammed the hat back on her head. "Did you see the fire in that woman's eyes? And the guy with the yellowed teeth looked like he'd turn his mother in for a shot of whiskey."

"You're right. Let's get out of here. We'll be safer and harder to spot inside the concert arena."

"Good point."

They walked briskly toward the underpass, taking turns checking behind them. Sadness settled around Alex, making her feet drag like she was wearing truck rims for sandals. There had to be a misunderstanding. Maybe there were two men looking for a hat. There was no way Ben would think she was thief, not after the dance and kiss they shared. She needed to find him to explain. A shiver ran up her spine. What if he had changed?

An elbow jostled against her hip, a forearm brushed her shoulder and she moved closer to

Shellie as the gravel path filled with people. Everyone condensed as the crowd moved closer to the highway.

The cement underpass was like a wide mouth funnel. Chain link fencing prevented pedestrians from climbing the embankment and walking across the freeway. The only way to cross the highway was to filter into the cement tunnel and go under the road. Everywhere, people were headed back—with an hour in-between performers there was just enough time for them to run back, grab a quick beer and something to eat before heading back over.

It was almost impossible to move in the direction of the concert bowl. Those trying were smashed into a single file line. Alex stood in front of Shellie, waiting for her turn. The crowd swelled. *Might as well be a salmon swimming upstream.* Bumped from behind, she took a step forward to keep her balance and the next thing she knew she was in the underpass.

Jostled this way and that, she shook her head and tried to back pedal, her hands instinctively reaching out for space. The tunnel was wall-to-wall people going in the opposite direction. She couldn't see how she could ever get to the other side. Instead of being spit back out, she got sucked further in.

Crap! She looked wildly around. Everyone was shoving and shouting, their voices echoing off the heavy cement walls. What was wrong with these people? Adrenaline rushed through her veins, her heart hammered. Everyone was nuts. Didn't they realize that someone could get hurt?

Pushed hard from behind, her face was suddenly crammed into the back of a hot, sweaty T-shirt. She wrestled her arms up from her side and placed them on the guy's waist. Sheer determination and strength helped her create a pocket of space to suck in hot, clammy air.

This is ridiculous! Surely, someone was going to fall and get trampled to death. Half-way through the tunnel, she took another breath and tried to remain calm. Wasn't there anyone to help? And where was Shellie?

She searched amongst the moving heads, then squinted. *No way.* Not three feet from her was Ben. "Hey!" she shouted in disbelief. "Ben!"

He turned and his eyes locked with hers. She pushed her feet into the pavement trying to dig in, but it was useless. Frustration surged. *"Ben!"*

Pushed from behind again, she staggered forward, their gazes torn apart.

"No!" Her voice blended into the noise as Ben disappeared from view.

Unshed tears blurred her vision. She blinked continuously. *Where did he go? And where was Shellie?* Her stomach churned. *Nothing had better have happened to her.*

Her grip on the man ahead of her tightened. She was not going to fall, she would not be trampled. She needed to get out and find Shellie.

Fresh air rushed over her face and she gulped as her fingers relaxed their grip. A quick side-step brought her to the side of the over-crowded path. Her heart pounded as she forced her eyelids into a more natural state.

Alex jumped up and down hoping to spot Shellie coming out of the underpass. As quickly as the crowds surged, they thinned. *Where was she? Did I miss her?*

Suddenly, she caught sight of the red T-shirt. "Thank God." Alex rushed forward and threw an arm around her friend. "Are you okay?"

"That was awful." Shellie trembled. "I don't ever want to go through there again."

Relief swept through Alex. Besides being pale, Shellie looked fine. She had no idea what she'd do if anything happened to her best friend.

Alex looped her arm over her friend's shoulders as they walked to the entrance of the concert bowl. There was a line to get in as the security guards checked purses and wristbands, but thankfully, there weren't more than a dozen people waiting and everyone was orderly.

"I've never been so frightened," said a pale mom with a backpack in one hand and her daughter gripped in the other. "I thought for sure someone was going to be killed."

A man with wisps of grey hair and plaid shorts clung to his wife and bobbed his balding head. "We won't be coming back. It's gotten out of hand."

The security guard waved everyone in their group through. "You can go," he said, not bothering to check bags and barely glancing at the passes on the lanyards.

Alex watched the older couple as they shuffled toward the front of the stage to the reserved seating area. He was so gentle and caring and the wife watched him with infinite tenderness. Her gaze clung to the pair, hoping she'd be lucky enough to find love, and fortunate enough to grow old with someone special.

She turned her attention back to Shellie, and noticed her friend's pallor. *Oh crap!* Her eyes darted around the starlet's face, hoping her friend wasn't going to faint. She steered her closer to the grass. If she were to drop, she didn't want her to land in the middle of a dirt-packed path.

She had no idea what to do; the only advice she could remember hearing was to have the victim put their head between their knees, which was worthless if the person was standing or lying down.

"Let's eat," Alex suggested, only because she'd heard her mom say it at least a million times. Her fingers tingled with the need to trace her heart tattoo.

Hollywood was speechless for once, but she nodded.

"Come on." Alex steered her past the wooden storefronts, where she took notice of what everyone was offering—ice cream, turkey legs, tacos, mini donuts, corn dogs, T-shirts, cowboy boots, hats, bumper stickers, beads and beer.

Shellie pointed to the turkey leg stand and Alex led the way.

"Aren't you going to get one?" Shellie asked.

The scent of the roast turkey made her stomach grumble and mouth water. "I saw Ben again," she confessed, shaking her head. "In the tunnel. He was walking away from the concert. What if he turned around? What if he's coming back to me?"

Shellie slid out from under Alex's arm. "So, you're never going to eat?"

"No. It's just, if he found someone else, I want him to be filled with regrets—not with images of a woman with turkey grease dribbling off her chin. That is not going to get him to think, 'I can't believe I let her get away.'"

Shellie shrugged. "I'd rather have a man know what he saw was what he got. I want to be liked for who I am. I have no desire to be a perfect, plastic, cookie cutter woman mimicking the models and actresses." Shellie scratched her chest then handed her money over to the older man in the white, stained apron behind the counter.

"Enjoy," he said, handing over a hefty hunk of meat.

Alex rolled her eyes and moved closer as they walked from the stand. "Kind of hard to be like everyone else...when your boobs are blue."

"Ha, ha." Shellie leaned against the side of the building, huddling in a sliver of shade.

While her friend made smacking sounds, Alex

turned her attention to the crowd. Hollywood didn't understand because she always had boyfriends—and now she had Joe. She crossed her arms over her chest. She'd been a grease monkey long enough to know that men didn't get turned on by the grime beneath her fingernails or the collection of wrenches in her toolbox.

Mmmmmm, two hard-bodied, bare-chested cowboys sporting matching grins caught her attention. They had cowboy hats, tight low-slung jeans, treasure trails and a dozen strands of beads around their necks. She poked her friend and nodded in their direction when two ladies shimmied up and started to dance around the cowboys. A moment later, the gals grabbed the edges of their shirts and flashed the stunned studs. The men staggered backward, their Adam's apples bobbing along with their eyes.

Alex's eyes widened and she nudged Shellie with her shoulder. "Don't you get any ideas about flashing your blue boobies for beads."

"And you wonder why I didn't want to tell you." Her friend's hair and hips swished on the way to the trash can. She tossed in the bone. "Aren't you coming? I thought we'd go to the same spot you sat in last year."

Alex walked over and handed her friend a spare napkin. "I don't know, maybe we should find a better spot." She had enough confrontations for one weekend. "I'm thinking I'll feel better if I can sit with my back to a wall."

"Chicken." Hollywood did a round the world with the napkin stuck to her chin. She tucked her hands under her armpits, flapped her arms and walked in circles making clucking sounds.

"Fine." Alex gave in. "It's your life if you want to take your chances sitting with a hat-thieving, man-stealing woman, but I'm not going anywhere with

92

you until you pull the napkin from your face."

The chicken stopped her clucking to imitate a boxer knocking the napkin from her chin. "For you, I'd take them all on."

Alex gave her a hip check. "Come on, Kung Fu Shellie. Let's go find a place to stand." *She's crazy.* But that's what she loved about her friend; she was a *free spirit.*

The number of people amazed her; there had to be twice as many as last year. She envied their freedom as the crowd swayed to the music, and wished *she* could let the music take her away. But she couldn't relax. Every few minutes, her head swiveled to survey those around her. With every redhead sighting, she held her breath and sent up a silent prayer that Ben wouldn't be attached to this one. So far, she had been lucky and a small sense of relief whooshed out of her on a long exhaled breath.

As the sun dropped lower in the sky, the lights came on, but her mood got lower with no sign of Ben whatsoever. With only an hour left before the headliners, Alex noticed Shellie looking a little pale. "Hey, maybe we should start heading back. I bet Joe has a fire going and I am getting cold."

Shellie rubbed her temples. "But they haven't even started the big stars yet...are you sure?"

She held out her arm with goose bumps as proof, then looped it through her friend's.

"But what about Ben?"

Alex forced a note of confidence into her voice. "If he was here, I would have found him by now." And, for the first time, the thought of Ben didn't bring a smile to her lips. The way her luck was going, he was probably in the corner dancing with his redhead.

At the end of the weekend would she be leaving empty handed—no Ben, no hat and no dreams left to keep her company?

Chapter Eight

Ben was seriously going to do bodily harm to Patrick if he didn't stop getting Julia drunk. One minute he was dancing with the crazy redhead at the concert bowl and the next, Ben was walking her back to the campsite, stopping to hold up her hair as she vomited in the bushes. It had taken forever to get her back and lying down in the tent.

"Julia," he whispered to the moaning body stretched out on the sleeping bag. "I'm going to take a walk. Here's some water." He set the plastic bottle down next to her. "Laurie and Mike are out by the fire if you need anything."

"Sorry, cowboy," she moaned.

"Maybe you'll learn not to play games with pirates."

She moaned louder and he carefully backed out of the tent. The best thing to do was let her sleep it off.

He walked over to the cooler, opened the lid and took out a beer. "I think I'll go for a walk while Julia recovers."

Mike made a move to get up. Laurie's blond curls bounced as she reached up and grabbed him. "You're not going anywhere."

Ben laughed and headed to the road. "See ya."

He kicked a rock as the muscles between his shoulder blades tightened. He could be wearing his hat and heading back to see Rascal Flatts right now—if Patrick or Julia would have had enough common sense to grab the Stetson when they ran into Alex.

He took a long pull. Patrick wouldn't say much other than to confirm Alex had the hat with her. Julia, on the other hand, had a lot to say—and none of it good.

She was laughing and telling her friend that she could get the cowboy back anytime she wanted, Julia had relished telling him. *I heard her tell her friend she'd play the field this weekend and if nothing better came along, would lure you back with the hat.*

Ben's stomach tightened. How could he have been so wrong? Last year he was certain she was a no frills type of gal—down to Earth, honest and real. From the glimpse he'd gotten of her at the underpass, she was still beautiful, but something was different and he couldn't put his finger on it.

If he'd only wanted the Barbie doll type, he would have settled down by now. And if he wanted sass and attitude, he wouldn't have told Julia that it wasn't going to work between them. He'd taken Patrick's advice and went with the 'rebound love never worked' argument. Women always claimed they wanted honest, but he couldn't look Julia in the eyes and tell her he just wasn't into her, or that he didn't want a woman who got drunker than he did.

With the last sip of his beer leaving a sour taste in his mouth, he slammed the bottle into a nearby garbage container. The sound of glass breaking gave him little satisfaction. Something had to give. He jammed his hands into his pockets and started down a path shadowed in a canopy of overhanging tree branches.

For a year, the image of her lips, the tint to her green eyes and the touch of her fingertips had flashed behind his closed eyelids. Now, here she was at Country Time, and he was still unable to reach out and touch her. His stomach coiled tighter with each missed opportunity. It was like standing in the batter's box, watching the ball sail by and hearing the umpire yell, 'Strike three!'

His pace slowed. Something just didn't feel right. He thought about the first time he saw her this weekend. Her lovely, long, lean arms held a towel to a woman's head as they drove away in a golf cart. It had taken him by surprise, yet she was everything he remembered. He hoped she'd stop, call out his name, but when their eyes met she'd glanced away. Had she even thought of him this past year? The thing that puzzled him the most was why she hadn't asked the driver to wait. It was like she was in a hurry to get away. A slight smile, a tiny wave, the hat was worth at least that much. A nod or brief acknowledgment that he existed, that she remembered him...but no, nothing.

He pulled his hands from his pockets and slapped a mosquito off his neck. The heels of his boots dragged through the gravel as his steps stumbled along with his thoughts. His stomach tightened and his breath became shallow as he recalled the image of Alex's large, frightened eyes clinging to him in the underpass. His heart was at odds with his thoughts and others' interpretations.

She had looked like a kitten that had wandered into a coral of wild horses, and he'd wanted nothing more that to dash over, scoop her up and remove her from harm's way.

The image of her in his arms spun him back to last year when he first asked her to dance. Her smile had been so sweet and warm. She had been willing in his arms, and a shiver of joy rode his spine when they fell so easily into step. Back then, her dazzling green eyes had held determination, her touch a strength and tenderness, and a confidence, that didn't come from a fancy French manicure, designer dresses or expensive perfumes. He had waited so long to find someone who was *real*. Then he had his dreams and hat snatched away in a blink of an eye.

His chest and throat tightened. It was the first time he allowed himself to remember so vividly and now he wished he hadn't. He swallowed and shoved the thoughts of her aside, forcing himself to think of Dustin and how happy he'd be to finally wear the special hat Ben had made sure he'd gotten autographed for him. He could see himself pushing his little brother on the swing and Dustin's joyous clapping and laughter. The thought pulled his lips up from their frown.

His mind wandered like his boots as he went up and down the dirt trails, trying to distance himself from thoughts of Alex.

The music from the concert bowl drifted over the speakers as Rascal Flatts hit the stage. For the cost of the tickets, he should be standing in front of that stage cheering instead of looking for someone he wasn't even sure he wanted to find.

That's it. His boot hit the ground hard. If she didn't show up by the end of the night, he was done looking for her. He was here to have a good time and all he had done so far was make himself miserable.

He glanced up at the sound of other footsteps on the gravel. Two women approached—one of them wore a cowboy hat.

Oh shit! The air whooshed from his lungs and he tipped from the waist as if he had been sucker punched. His arms clutched his stomach as he straightened up.

They stopped and stared...she took one step closer.

Alex.

His heart plummeted and went on the rollercoaster ride of his life.

Wide-eyed and innocent, with a beacon-bright smile and steps that were steady and sure, she slipped the Stetson off. Her brown hair looked different as long red manicured fingernails smoothed the silky strands into place.

His jaw slacked. She was amazingly beautiful, so much more than he had remembered. Last year she had been a diamond in the rough—this year, stunning, radiant and polished. She certainly wouldn't have any trouble attracting a man. His lips stuck to his teeth and his lungs burned for air when she smiled and skipped closer.

He gained control of his body and slammed his mouth shut. Who was this woman? The sweet angel of last year, or was he seeing the real woman, the teasing and cruel thief?

Alex's eyes lit up like a Christmas tree as she extended the hat.

He staggered back, certain she was about to step into his arms. He wasn't ready for her to touch him, not yet, not in this painful confusion.

Her gaze dimmed. "I've waited for the chance to return your hat. I was worried I wouldn't be able to find you..." Her voice faltered and she reached out a perfectly manicured hand toward him.

Ben stuffed his right hand into the pocket of his jeans. She finally dropped her hand. With a raised brow, he let his gaze roam up and down this familiar stranger. "Here I thought you were avoiding me." He couldn't help the sarcasm that dripped from his voice, couldn't match the woman from last year to the polished beauty before him. "Zooming past me at the showers and then running from me at the railroad crossing. When all you were really doing was trying to find me?" He grabbed for the hat. His fingers brushed against hers and his heart slammed into his chest as instant desire sparked in the pit of his stomach.

Why did she have to be so damn sexy and beautiful? *And deceitful, remember?* Even so, he wanted nothing more then to run his fingers through the soft, golden brown hair that brushed against her smooth shoulders. To have his hands run down the length of her back and settle against the small curve just above the swell of her butt. To pull her close and have the fullness of her breasts pressed up against his chest. To once again experience the sweetness of her kisses.

She stepped closer, filling the gap between them. "Ben, I want—," her voice pleaded.

He was drowning in the pools of her eyes and clenched his jaw shut as the hairs on the back of his neck stood up with the remembered comments from Julia. *Yeah, you want me, but only because you hadn't found anything better, right?* Anger flared and he narrowed his eyes, adding aloud, "Your parents should have named you *Jezebel*."

"What?" Her eyebrows rose as confusion clouded her eyes. She blinked. "I know this looks bad, but I can explain."

He ignored the plea in her voice, put the hat on his head and swallowed. He took a step backward as she came forward.

"Ben, please listen." Her voice trembled. "I can explain. I want you—"

He put his hands on her shoulders to prevent her from coming any closer, but as soon as his palms touched her skin, his hands started shaking. Something was wrong, different, he could see it in her eyes. And the way she looked? This couldn't be the same angel his heart had longed for—had everyone else really seen what he couldn't?

"I don't want to hear it. I already know," he snapped, delving into his self-loathing and fortifying his resolve. "You stole my hat—a hat I was going to give my little brother."

"No, that's not how it was." Alex pressed against his hands and tried to move in closer, her eyes rimmed in tears.

"Yeah, right." He dropped his hands to his sides and looked away. Taking a deep breath, he tried to quiet the anger that threatened to bubble up and over. "I don't need an explanation. I was there." Ben took the hat from his head and held it up. "Remember? I put this hat, *my hat,* on your head. And then you left without a 'good-bye' or a 'see you around.'" He tapped the brim of the Stetson against her chest. "That's what I get for thinking we had something special. Boy, was I wrong! To you it was all a joke—"

He stopped as her facial features froze. The stone-cold gaze sent a shiver down his spine.

"That's *not* how it was." She tossed her words at him like rocks, her hands clenched into tight fists.

He gingerly placed the hat on his head; he'd teach her to toy with him. "Sweetheart," his voice dripped like honey on a hot biscuit. "It doesn't matter. I have all that I want from you now...the hat. It's over."

"Y-y-you." Her voice shook with accusation, along with her body, as she backhanded a tear from her cheek.

His brows dropped low, not sure if she was going to cold cock him or sob. He watched hypnotically as a single tear streamed to her chin.

His stomach clenched. How dare she cry? His insides turned into one giant Jell-O shot. She'd played him for a fool once; he wasn't about to let it happen again. "Save your crocodile tears for someone who'll appreciate them...I don't." He spit the words out.

She stood as still as a statue. Instead of feeling vindicated, he felt like crap, like he'd ripped a bone from a puppy's mouth. Her eyes brimmed with unshed tears.

He hated that his arms ached to hold her close, to at least brush the tear from her. *Don't let her make a fool out of you two years in a row. You'll never be able to face your friends again.*

Damn. Maybe there was a reasonable explanation, a small voice inside his head whispered. *No,* he screamed back. *Fool! Idiot! She's nothing but an actress practicing her drama school antics.* She had to be; it was the only validation he had for his year's worth of pent up anger...right?

Ben turned slowly around. Before he took a step, his body paused, and he willed her fingertip to brush against his body...just one single touch...*and I'll turn around. Prove me wrong and I'll turn around.*

Nothing.

His heels kicked up dirt. He was done waiting. He placed one foot in front of the other, while his thoughts spun and his stomach churned. *I'm not looking back.* Anger rumbled through his whole body. *What type of woman played with a man's heart and head?* The type of gal he didn't want to get involved with. He didn't want a teasing drama queen in his life; he wanted a woman who was real. He thought he had found her in Alex...

He couldn't have been more wrong.

With every step he justified his words and actions. He tried to tick off the reasons why he wasn't attracted to Alex, but when the campsite came into view, the only thing unticked was 'thief'.

Ben snatched the hat from his head and inhaled. The hat smelled like a field of wildflowers in bloom on a warm, breezy, summer day. Alex's scent. He almost moaned aloud. There was no way he could walk around all weekend with that sweet reminder of his foolishness.

No! There was nothing natural about Alex. She was nothing more than a cheaply perfumed plastic rose. He clung to the image and yanked open the door to his truck, angrily throwing the hat on the front seat. The slammed door echoed through the quiet campsite, the likes of a ghost town with a lone piece of charred wood smoking in the campfire ring and empty chairs all around. He slunk into one and stretched out his legs. The sound of giggling erupted from Mike and Laurie's tent and grated on his nerves. His hand grabbed his rib cage as his forearm tried to cover the raw gnawing pain in his stomach. Unable to sit, he paced the grass then checked on Julia. She was still moaning, but not as loudly.

"Did you get the hat, cowboy?" she mumbled.

"Yeah."

"You okay?"

"Sure, go back to sleep." He ducked out of the tent and ambled back to the campfire. He flopped onto a lawn chair, leaned over and turned on the portable radio.

With one arm resting over his eyes, he began a long night of refusing to let the conversation or images of Alex become imbedded in his brain. He worked on saying the alphabet backwards, shifted numerous times to get comfortable and rubbed his stomach as he tried to quiet the churning and gurgling. His mind said the whole Alex thing was behind him, but the hurt and disappointment in his heart felt like it did last year when he returned with his friends only to find her gone.

He scrubbed his brow, trying to remove the image of big green eyes glistening with tears. What in the world was that all about? *It was only a flippin' hat.* Sure he'd been a little gruff, but not *that* hard.

Ben tightened his arms across his chest and pushed the image away. He couldn't allow himself to be lured back in. Once was more than his pride would allow.

Chapter Nine

Alex swallowed, forcing the pain deep down inside, blinking and willing the tears not to fall. She would not cry over him. He wasn't worth it. She should have stayed home changing oil.

"Are you okay?" Shellie's voice was full of concern.

Alex nodded, not knowing who she was madder at—Ben for being a jerk and not listening to her or herself for spending a year of her life pinning away for a loser. She stomped a foot. "He wouldn't even listen. And *Jezebel!* Can you believe that?"

"What do you think he meant?" Shellie asked.

Frustration and repressed anger throbbed through her limbs. Her feet slapped the trail as she started back for their campsite. "Obviously, he thinks I'm evil and scheming."

Her friend stopped dead in her tracks bringing Alex to a halt as well. "We have to go after him. We have to explain."

Alex walked on, dragging Shellie with her. "No way. You heard him. He already has his mind made up." Alex turned and shouted into the darkness. "Your parents should have named you Doubting Thomas!"

"Come on."

Shellie spun Alex around and pointed her in the direction of their tent.

She shook her arm loose, her hands balled into fists. She needed to keep a lid on her emotions. The last thing she wanted was for him, or anyone else, to see how this affected her. She'd put on a happy face, smile through her tears and laugh like it's going out of style...she had to, to survive it. "Can you believe this! All through high school I had to put up with guys calling me a grease monkey and now he thinks he can call me a Jezebel?"

"I'm sure he didn't mean it. He obviously has no clue what happened."

"*Because he wouldn't listen.*" Alex tossed her hands high into the air. "For a whole year, I've been feeling sorry for him. The only thing he lost was his stupid hat and now he's got it back. I lost my mom and my dad lost his legs. Things we'll *never* get back."

"When you put it like that—"

"To be so...so...uncompassionate—he's not who I thought he was." How could she have been so wrong?

Shellie squeezed her tight then danced out in front of her, a grin stretched ear to ear. "Maybe it's time you found yourself a new cowboy...or maybe a race car driver. Hey! How about pirates?" She drew an imaginary sword and stabbed the air. "Or better yet, maybe Joe has a friend."

Against her will the corners of her lip tipped up into a smile. The starlet was trying so hard to make this better. "Yeah, maybe a doctor or a lawyer," she mumbled, then her chin shot up. She'd love to see the look on the cowboy's face if she walked by on the elbow of some hot, rich guy.

Shellie strutted around, trying to imitate a variety of professions and she couldn't hold back her laughter any longer when the starlet did an impression of what Alex could only assume was a baseball player.

Her friend chuckled and continued a macho scratch of her crotch. "I don't know if we can find you a ball player or a lawyer, but if *you* fell, we could take you to the hospital where a handsome, single doctor would take one look at your scraped knee and fall madly in love with you."

It was impossible to stay in a foul mood with Shellie around. "Did you learn that in Girl Scouts, too?" Alex teased.

"Some things we just can't divulge. My lips are sealed."

The starlet mimed her mouth locked and they walked in silence the rest of the way. When they reached their campsite, Alex was relieved to see Joe. She didn't know how much longer she could keep up the happy façade, and Joe would be a good distraction so Shellie wouldn't fret over her.

"I wasn't sure if you girls had eaten." Joe poked a stick into the fire, shuffling around packages of tinfoil. "So, I cooked up some hobo meals."

"They're my favorite." Shellie beamed. "I haven't had one since Girl Scouts." Wide eyed, she clamped a hand over her mouth.

Joe laughed. "*You* were a Girl Scout?"

Shellie hid her face behind her hands.

"It's okay," Joe added gently.

She lowered her hands, exposing pink-stained cheeks. "Yeah, until I graduated from high school, just one of those nerdy girls."

"Now we share a secret." He held up two fingers. "I was a Boy Scout."

Alex plopped down in the chair. Hollywood and the leading man continued to chat, but she gave up on following their conversation about scouting events and camping trips. At the moment, she was knee-deep in her own pity party and wished she had never come back to Country Time. For weeks she warned herself that the weekend might not lead to the two of them together—but not once did she ever think it would end this way, that he would think her a tease and a thief. All she'd wanted was a happy ending. The kind where she walked off into the sunset with the guy. *Or he stood howling at the moon wanting me back.* The thought of Ben being a sorry cowboy lightened the weight on her shoulders.

Her jaw clenched. But he wasn't sorry. He didn't even act like he had liked her.

Reality sucked.

She was so lost in thought that when Joe set a tinfoil meal in front of her she jumped.

"Shellie mentioned you hadn't eaten. It's not much, but you should eat something."

He really did have kind eyes. "Thank you. It smells delicious." She unwrapped the foil and peered at the burger and potatoes. Taking a bite, she nodded and made the appropriate murmuring sounds. With a mouth full of bitterness, she could only assume the meal was tasty.

"I wish I would have brought all the stuff to make s'mores or pudgy pies," Shellie said between mouthfuls. "We used to use white bread, canned pie filling and metal plates to cook them over an open fire..."

"Didn't they get hot?" Alex asked.

"They were on long handles," Shellie clarified with a roll of eyes.

Joe winked. "Easy bake ovens for Girl Scouts."

Shellie was up on her feet, hands placed firmly on her hips. "I suppose the Boy Scouts were too primitive to use modern day cooking utilities."

Joe laughed and leaned closer to Shellie. "I'm thinking you girls had the right idea. I'd love a pudgy pie." He gave her a peck on the cheek. "I've got a surprise for you."

Shellie's eyes were as big as silver dollars when Joe handed her a sack. She reached in and pulled out a bag of marshmallows, graham crackers and chocolate bars. In her squealed excitement she knocked over a chair, and if not for Joe's quick reflexes, it would have wound up in the fire.

Hollywood wrapped her arms around her leading man's neck and kissed him hard and loud. Shellie looked like she had just received the moon wrapped with a bow. Alex's heart hurt.

"Let's see if we can find some sticks," she sighed. "Come on, Alex."

"I think I'll sit here and keep an eye on the fire. I'm not that hungry."

"You have to have a s'more," she said dejectedly.

"I will."

Alex tried for a smile as they wandered toward the trees, but as soon as they disappeared, the corners of her mouth plummeted. She tried to lose herself in the song that was playing on her neighbor's radio, but it was useless. Her thoughts kept going back to Ben, his words echoing, *We had something special.*

Her head pounded. He had felt it too. Last year wasn't her overactive imagination. His words replayed over and over, *something special.*

They did have something. Her heart plummeted. If only he had let her explain, they could be wrapped in each other's arms.

Her pride rose to the surface. *Thief? Jezebel? How dare he! He'll be sorry he didn't listen. I'm lucky to be rid the self-centered cowboy.*

Her heart continued to yo-yo, one moment, remembering how his fingers had brushed hers, how her heart had jolted at the site of him and the next, watching his brown eyes fill with accusations.

She couldn't believe he had called her Jezebel. She hated being called names. Why wouldn't he listen? Ben's words drifted back to her, *I thought we had something special...*

They only brought more confusion.

Twenty minutes later and still lost in her own thoughts, she barely looked up when Joe and Shellie carried three long sticks to the fire. Even so, Alex didn't miss Joe's telltale blush. She wondered what they had found first, sticks or kisses. To be honest, she was surprised they remembered to bring back sticks at all. No wonder the Boy and Girl Scouts never merged.

She stood and stretched. "I'm beat."

"You sure? I think I'll stay up and keep Joe company for awhile." Shellie nodded and winked as she poked a marshmallow onto a stick.

"Good night, you two."

Alex crawled into the tent and across the canvas bottom floor to her sleeping bag. She sprawled out and stared into the darkness. Her thoughts joined her shadowed vision and took a darker turn of their own.

He's going to pay for calling me Jezebel.

****

The sound of birds chirping had Alex shaking her head. She couldn't believe she'd actually fallen asleep. While stretching, the events from last night flashed and burned like a smoldering cigarette in the pit of her stomach. Her lids fluttered open as Ben's discarded words replayed in her head once again. She rolled over and buried her face in the pillow.

Shellie nudged her shoulder. "Are you sleeping?"

With eyes closed, she flipped on her back and responded, "Yeah..."

"Isn't Joe amazing? Marshmallows and hobo meals—how romantic!"

Alex tightened her eyelids until her cheeks crinkled.

"And when he kissed me..."

A hard poke invaded her side. Reluctantly, she opened one eye.

"Don't you think that was sweet? He thinks we're perfect...like s'mores," her friend gushed.

"Let me guess, you're the cracker." Alex rolled away from her gleeful friend, but that didn't deter

Shellie from gushing for five more minutes about Joe.

"His kiss feels so right." Shellie tapped out a rhythm on her arm. "Have you heard a word I said?"

"Ow." Alex rolled onto her back. "If I say he's the best and you make a great couple, will you quit poking me and let me go back to sleep?"

"You can't sleep all day. It's nine o'clock and the music starts at noon. What do you want to do?"

Alex tossed her arm over her eyes. "Nothing. I'm going to lie here until it's time to go home. I returned the hat, my mission is complete."

Shellie grabbed hold of her hands and yanked so hard Alex's shoulders flew from the ground, while her head bobbed backwards. "I am not going to let you to hide in this tent."

"I'm not hiding. To be hiding someone would have to be looking for me and he's *not* looking for me." Alex yanked her arms from Shellie's grip, fell back down to her sleeping bag and covered her eyes with her arm. "Besides, if I did get up and my path crossed Ben's, I'd be tempted to blacken both his eyes. Sleeping sounds so much better then going to jail."

"Screw Ben. This is supposed to be *your* weekend, your last hurrah, remember? Yes, you were hoping he was part of it and I can't fix that...but I'm not going to let you spend your big weekend alone in this tent either."

"Fine, you can stay in here with me because I'm not going out."

"Humph!" Shellie stormed from the tent.

Alex gave a shudder as a sigh of relief whooshed from her lungs. Before a thought could form in her head, though, Shellie crawled back in the tent.

"You are going to get up and take a shower. Now, missy!"

Alex snorted. "You forgot to stomp your foot. If

you're going to act like a spoiled starlet you're going to have to do better than that."

"Well, today I'm a Drill Sergeant. Now, march!" She barked out the orders. "On your feet!"

"Go away."

"No, I won't."

Something cold and gooey ran down her scalp. Alex bolted upright, swiping at the substance. "What the—"

"Relax. It's only shampoo."

She darted a finger towards Shellie's forehead. "That bump shook your brains loose—you're acting crazy!"

"Maybe, but now you *need* a shower," her ex-friend said simply.

Alex narrowed her eyes. "Here's the deal." She spoke each word slowly and clearly. "I'll go to the shower with you. *If* you promise to leave me alone."

"Deal." Shellie bubbled and gushed like she had made the cheerleading tryouts.

Alex shook her head. Her friend was up to something. She sat up and somberly stared into Shellie's eyes. "Don't think you can cross your fingers and break your promise. I plan on returning back to the tent and sleeping until it's time to go home."

"Okay." Shellie stuffed things in a backpack. "Look, I'm even helping you get ready, shampoo, sexy little underwear, hot white T-shirt..."

"Don't forget a paper bag to put over my head. Or should I just tell everyone I was slimed by a Girl Scout?"

Shellie tossed her a baseball cap and bandana. "Pick."

Alex smashed the cap on her head and emerged from the tent, blinking as her eyes adjusted to the bright sunlight. Just her luck, not a cloud in sight. She had been hoping for rain, lots of it, so much that they'd have to cancel the concert and she could go home.

"Come on." Shellie tugged her to the road.

"You're going the wrong way. The VIP showers are this way."

"Those are too far away."

"Yeah, well I don't want to run into Ben. I saw him at the semi-trailer showers yesterday."

They both stood with their feet firmly planted.

Shellie let out a long sigh. "There was a time when I thought you were the bravest person I knew, but the polish on your nails and highlights in your hair have changed more than your outward appearance. What happened to the Alex that wasn't afraid of anything—who was proud of the dirt under her fingernails?"

The anger that had been holding Alex rigid and upright drained from her shoulders and they slumped forward. A year ago, she would never have sulked in a tent—Shellie was right. Her fingers sprayed across her stomach. There was no fire in her belly. Somehow, she had gone from fearless to fearful, constantly worrying and second-guessing her every move. Where was her confidence? Deep within, a tiny spark ignited and she stood taller. "I'm a grease monkey who has been accepted into college."

Her friend jabbed her arm. "Yeah!"

"I can turn a wrench *and* a man's head."

"Yes you can!"

"Yeah." She wrapped Shellie in a hug. "What would I do without you?"

Her best friend slapped her back. "This is going to be a much better year. Come on." She moved from the embrace and started skipping down the road, calling out a greeting to everyone they passed.

"Go right." She bumped Shellie and pointed to the two large white tractor-trailers. "Down there."

The facilities looked different from the

permanent women's bathroom at the VIP campgrounds they had showered in yesterday. Besides having tires and metal steps leading up to the door, there were men and women in the lines waiting outside each trailer. Shellie walked over and Alex fell into step behind her

"So, how does this work?" Her obnoxiously cheerful friend asked the woman with a head full of blond curls standing in front of them.

"Each trailer has five private showers in a room just a little bit bigger than a closet. The water usually isn't warm and—"

"Wait." Shellie pointed to the men in line ahead of them. "These aren't semi private showers? They do have doors?"

The woman brushed a honey curl from her sleepy eyes and laughed. "Yesterday, I had the same concerns until the woman in front of me explained how it worked."

"How long have you been in line?" Shellie continued to pepper the poor woman with questions.

"About ten minutes. The showers are open from seven in the morning until ten at night and there's always a line. I figure we've another fifteen minutes or so before our turn comes up."

Great, more waiting. Just what she didn't want. The promise to be brave and more like her old self was forgotten as a foul mood settled around her. Alex was certain at any moment she was going to start growling and showing her teeth. She tried to force the corners of her mouth up into a partial smile but failed. The best she could do was keep her lips pressed tightly together. But a moment later, her upper lip curled and her eyebrows dropped dangerously low.

Ben descended down the trailer steps. His stone-cold brown eyes were clouded in anger and focused directly on her.

The hairs on her arms bristled, her lip drew up into a snarl. What right did *he* have to be mad? *He got his damn hat.*

His gaze traveled slowly over her body. Alex's heart beat faster. Her body might be weak, but her mind was strong. Her lazy gaze moved from the frown in his brow, down to the tips of his toes and back to a spot beside his right eye. The words he said last night played in her head. *It doesn't matter. I have the hat now. It's all over.*

Anger narrowed her eyes, flared her nostrils and burned the back of her throat. With valiant effort, she shook her head and rolled her eyes, dismissing him like yesterday's news.

"Thanks for the shampoo, Laurie." His voice was too cheery and exuberant.

From under her lashes Alex watched him hand a bottle to the curly-haired woman.

Her heart pounded harder and her mind screamed louder. *If he was any type of man, he'd at least say, 'Thanks for returning the hat.' Or apologize for his obnoxious behavior the night before.*

She hadn't meant to glance up into his brown eyes. He blinked, and for half-a-second, she wondered if he could read her mind. Her heart paused along with her breath. *Maybe...*

Then his eyelids narrowed and his lip curled up. "What? Stealing my hat wasn't enough? Now, you have to stalk me?"

Chapter Ten

The pounding in her ears was so loud she could no longer hear her thoughts. She pushed Shellie aside, zeroed in on Ben's upper lip and cocked her arm back.

"No!" Her friend's nails dug into her flesh.

Her fist barely brushed his chin. He backed up a step, surprise evident on his face. From the corner of her eye she saw heads turning, but this time, she didn't care how big a scene she made.

Alex yanked her arm free from Shellie's death grip and fumed at the cheesy smile that flashed across Ben's rugged features.

She poked his naked chest. Her finger repeatedly found its mark. "You conceited. Ignorant. *Jerk*," she said with a final stab. "If I never see you again, that would be just fine by me."

"Well, at least I'm not *a thief.*" His index finger poked against her collarbone.

She slapped his hand away. "I'm not a thief," she shouted and moved even closer.

His facial features could have been carved out of stone and his body solid as a brick wall. But he didn't intimidate her and she easily stood her ground.

"You stole my hat."

"I gave you your stupid hat back." Their noses were almost touching now. "You, *mister*, owe *me* an apology."

"You're right. I *am* sorry...sorry that I ever met you."

Her hands reflectively came up and she shoved, but he didn't move. "You're not half as sorry as I am. I wish *I* never met you!"

"You don't have to scream—I'm standing right in front of you. I can hear perfectly."

"Well, hear this, then." Her chest pushed against his. She wanted him out of her way and out of her life. "You're a jerk!" Someone wedged an arm between them. "What the—" Her snarl snapped off when she recognized the pirate's tattooed arm.

"Come on, you two. Break it up." Patrick eased Ben back a couple of steps.

"Oh no, trouble to the left," Shellie whispered in her ear.

From the corner of her eye, Alex caught a glimpse of the petite redhead. Her destination was clear as thin arms pumped the air and angry feet kicked up dirt. Alex's insides froze. If the woman got her hands on Patrick, she'd kill him—that much was evident from their last encounter at the showers. But, before she could blink, the chick rushed around the pirate, planted her hands on Alex's chest and shoved.

Alex stumbled backward. Before she could get her feet under her, the crazy bitch rushed forward and gave another shove. Alex's arms flailed as she tried to steady herself.

Strong arms shot out and wrapped around her waist, spinning her away from the angry woman.

Alex watched as Patrick wrapped an arm around the redhead's waist and hoisted her into the air. Her arms and legs thrashed. There was no doubt in Alex's mind this woman was out to hurt someone—and she seemed to be top on her list. She couldn't help but stare at the spectacle, and wonder what the pirate saw in that crazy woman.

Heat settled in her back causing her heart to clog in her throat. That left only one person close enough to pull her out of harm's way. Ben. His arms tightened around her and she twisted and strained. "Let me go."

His gripped loosened. "Don't worry. Julia's harmless." His breath warmed more than her neck as her feet ended up on solid ground. Instantly, she took a step to the side, her body cooling as fast as her heart.

"*Put me down,*" the evil chick screeched.

"Not until you agree to behave." Patrick tipped his head back, narrowly missing one of her flaying arms.

She pounded on his back. "Let me down. I warned that whore-bitch yesterday to leave my man alone."

Whore-bitch? That's it! I'm not going to let that crazy witch stand there and call me names. Alex lunged for the woman.

Patrick turned, shielding Julia. "Take her!" He shoved the redhead at Ben and blocked Alex. "I'm all for chick fights, unless I happened to be in-between them."

She strained against the confines of his arms.

Patrick rocked her gently. "Shhhhh, relax. It's going to be okay," he whispered.

Julia wrapped dramatic arms around Ben. "Kiss me, cowboy,"

Cowboy, not pirate. She'd had it all wrong— again. Alex averted her gaze; all the fight seeped out of her. Another woman kissing Ben was more then she could stomach. "It's okay. You can let go of me," she whispered in Patrick's ear.

"I don't want to." His hands trailed down her back and stopped on her hips.

"Please."

His hands shimmied back up to her shoulders and then slid down the length of her arms to capture her left hand. He flipped her palm up and raised it to his lips. "Patrick." He whispered across her skin. He kissed her palm and then closed her fingers. "Today my name is on your palm. Someday, I hope my name will be on your lips and in your heart."

Unable to help herself, she smirked at the pirate. He was sweet, charming and kind of cute. She only wished it was his gaze that caused her knees to go weak.

When the obnoxiously loud smacking sounds started, Alex turned back in Ben's direction, certain the two of them would be in the throws of love. Her eyes widened as Ben ripped the Velcro girlfriend from his chest.

Alex chuckled as Ben squirmed over the redhead's public display of affection. He caught sight of her and his eyebrows dropped dangerously low. She sucked in a breath as his cold glare silenced her laughter.

Patrick's fingertip traced the heart on her arm before he wrapped her in a hug. "Tomorrow, it will hurt less," he whispered. "But to get through today, you'll be in need of my services. I'd be more than happy to distract you. Look for me where you found me yesterday."

She spoke to Patrick while staring at Ben. "I might just do that."

His thumb brushed under her chin. "It would help if you looked at me when you spoke." She glanced briefly into his gaze and gave a quick nod.

Patrick gave her hand a long, lingering squeeze. "Okay then, I won't say good bye—I'll simply say, see you soon."

The smile she returned was genuine. *He was sweet*.

He walked up to the love birds and pushed them down the path.

In front of Shellie, the curly blonde stood with the shampoo bottle in her hands, her eyes and mouth propped opened. "Wow. So, *you're* the woman who shattered Ben's heart."

Alex's head swiveled. "No."

"He gave you his hat and asked you to wait," the blonde stated matter-of-factly.

Alex rolled her eyes and shouldered away from the woman. *Next she'll call me 'thief', too.*

"You know Ben?" Shellie asked.

Wait, did she say broke his heart?

"My husband Mike and Ben are best friends." She fixed her gaze on Alex. "Last year Ben had been so excited. I'd never seen him so ecstatic. He told us he had met the woman of his dreams. He dragged us all back to meet you...and you were gone." The blond stared long and hard. "If you could have seen his face, you wouldn't be standing here so smug today."

"Shower's open," the attendant hollered to the woman.

The blonde hesitated. "Ben's really a nice guy. You shouldn't have treated him like that." She flipped her hair, stormed around and strode up the stairs. Stopping half way, she turned and called out, "You don't deserve him."

Alex shook her head at the retreating back, wanting to defend herself, but a lump the size of a bowling ball had lodged itself in her throat.

Shellie slapped her back. "And here I worried you wouldn't find Ben. Now it seems you can't turn around without running into him, or someone he knows." She gave a heavy sigh and shook her head. "Small world."

Alex nodded.

"Next," called the attendant.

"I'll wait for you." Shellie rushed toward the stairs.

Alex stood in the silence, trying to sort it all out. Ben was with the crazy woman, and the pirate and the blonde woman were all his friends. *And besides*

Ben telling everyone I'm a thief, they all think I shattered his heart, yet no one wanted to listen to me. They already tried me and found me guilty.

By the time it was her turn to enter the facilities, her head was pounding. The shower was icy cold, but she didn't even mind. She scrubbed her body and wished the water could cool her thoughts, which refused to veer from her encounters with Ben. By the time she turned off the faucet, her skin glowed and her teeth chattered. Alex slipped back into her clothes and walked down the trailer steps to find Shellie standing in the shade of the trailer.

Silently, they strolled back to their campsite. Her heart was so heavy her feet dragged across the gravel like lead. Every step was an effort. All she wanted to do was go home, crawl into bed and pull the covers over her head.

A beautiful orange Monarch fluttered by and a small smile tugged at the corners of her mouth. A few minutes later the butterfly was back, although this time it continued to dance a few feet in front of her.

Her spirits lifted. *A message from mom?*

They were almost to camp when three young men walked by.

"Morning," they called out in unison, checking her and Shellie out from head to toe. From the flash of large grins, they must have passed inspection.

"Hello." At least someone desired her.

By the time Alex's feet danced into camp, her mood had lightened.

Shellie, on the other hand, dragged and barely managed to make it into a chair where she sprawled out. "I'm just going to close my eyes for a couple of minutes."

"You know, if you didn't insist on getting up so early you wouldn't be tired."

Alex quickly slipped into the tent. She pulled on

her favorite faded denim shorts and a red-and-white-checked cotton blouse. Her dad would tease her every time she wore it. *You must be desperate for clothes that you're wearing the kitchen table cloth.* She chuckled at the thought of his lame joke, grasping another positive in her negative day.

She skipped the make-up and braided her hair into pigtails. If Shellie wasn't going to let her hide out in the tent, then, from here on out, she wasn't here to impress, simply to enjoy the music.

When she stepped outside, her friend stretched and yawned. "Hey, you look like good old Alex."

"I'll take that as a complement."

Shellie stood and opened the cooler, popping a top on a diet soda. "Let's head over to the concert early. I want to see if I can get some beads for Edna."

Alex stuffed her hands into the pockets of her shorts. "You're not going to flash anyone, are you?"

"I thought about it, but decided it'd be less work to buy them, but if *you* wanted to—"

Alex yanked her hand from her pocket like she was trying to stop Harley when he gunned his fifty-five Buick into the garage stall for an oil change. Her palm slapped against air. "No way."

Giggling, Shellie held up her hand, fingers splayed. "Fine, give me five minutes and I'll be ready to go."

Alex plopped into a chair. *Only twenty-four hours to go.* Tomorrow at this time, everyone would be packing up. She shrugged, leaned back and closed her eyes. Not the ending she had envisioned, but then, maybe it was for the best. She'd be starting school after all and making a new life for herself.

"Wake up, sleepy head," Shellie's voice sang out. "I thought we could take a walk and tour some of the campsites."

"I just sat down," Alex groaned as she slowly

hefted herself out of the chair.

"Come on."

"All right."

Alex fell into step as Shellie immediately started a commentary. "Joe told me he's been doing security here for five years and every year it's a lot of the same people. Kind of like a cult thing. He mentioned that this was the biggest year yet."

The starlet's arms waved as if she were the model on a game show, pointing out a site that had been set up like an old time saloon and all. She showcased a watermelon patch, but instead of the fruit being on a vine, the melons were arrange on a green tarp and had various bottles of alcohol draining into them. A large sign hung at the entrance to the campsite: Watermelon Crawl at Noon Today.

Music blared from the radio, the site already buzzing with activity. It wouldn't be long before they started cutting up the fruit.

"Isn't it great?" Shellie bubbled. "Joe's working the first two shifts today, so, after Brooks and Dunn, he can hang out with us..."

Alex nodded, only half paying attention. She wanted to remain alert and didn't want to be blindsided by that crazed redhead. Slowly, they made their way to the underpass. Today, thankfully, only a couple of people trickled though the tunnel.

"I guess everyone else is sleeping or getting primed for later," Shellie offered.

At the entrance, Alex smiled brightly at the security guard. "Good morning," she said. "How's it going today?"

His teeth flashed and a dimple appeared on his right side. "Better. And yourself?"

"Better, too, thanks for asking." And it was true. No, she didn't want to run into anyone from Ben's little cluster, but the sun was shining and she started school next week. This was *her* weekend to let loose and have fun. As she forcefully ignored the big bruise on her heart, her steps lightened.

"You ladies have a nice day."

"Thank you," Alex said as she floated by.

Shellie gave her a small jab. "He was kind of cute."

"I'm telling Joe you're checking out other security guards."

Her friend blushed as she shoved Alex toward a storefront with beads and jewelry on display. "I wasn't looking for me. I was looking for *you*."

Alex stepped up on the wooden boardwalk. The scent of mini donuts and coffee was thick in the air.

Shellie walked into the store. Her fingers ran through strands of beads, and a moment later, she handed over five dollars for a dozen plastic strands of shiny green, gold, purple and red ones.

She held up her purchase. "Do you have a bag?"

"Aren't you going to wear them?" the clerk countered.

The starlet's eyes got larger, and she suddenly acted like the strands were a handful of snakes.

"For Pete's sake." Alex took the beads from Shellie's hand and put the strands one by one over her own head. "You don't think they clash with my red-and-white-checked shirt, do you?"

"You look ridiculous," Shellie said, grinning.

"Perfect."

Music from the nearby stage started up. "Come on! Taylor Swift is playing."

They hustled to a large clearing just on the other side of reserved seating where others had gathered to dance. Alex's hips swayed and she let her body and thoughts get lost in the music. A few songs later, fingertips brushed against her elbow.

"May I have this dance?" a gentleman with a handlebar mustache inquired.

"Uh, sure," she said, glancing beneath the brim of his large cowboy hat and into a pair of kind grey eyes.

He clasped her hand and held her at a respectable distance. He was light on his feet and moved her with confidence.

Shellie flashed past Alex's view and shouted, "Yee haw!"

The current dance partner who spun her friend might not have much finesse, but he certainly had enthusiasm. She laughed as Shellie spun faster.

The dance area filled with people who swung, stomped and swayed to the music. Alex felt a tap on her shoulder and the man holding her took a step back. "Thanks, miss," he said with a grin and released her hand. A lively cowboy grabbed it, immediately twirling her into a fast two-step. The more they spun, the bigger his grin grew, all mouth.

"Whoa!"

He let go of her hand and she spun out of control and crashed into the arms of yet another man. She clutched his waist and stood staring at the ground while she brought her eyes back into focus.

Strong arms tightened around her. An ignited fuse lit a brief tingle of sparks at the base of her tailbone seconds before a flash of fire raced to the top of her spine. Her head snapped up and their eyes met. *Ben*. What was going on?

Heat flooded her body.

His gaze held her tight while his arms relaxed. The touch from his hands was so light his fingers barely rested on her back.

She only needed to take a small step back and his hold would be broken. But, as she stared into the depth of his brown eyes, her rebellious body didn't want to go. A slight tremor ran from her shoulders to her heels. Slowly, her arms slid up and her hands clasped his shoulders. The heat from his skin singed her palms.

Brown eyes turned to velvet as his fingers swayed like wheat fields across her back.

She hardly dared to breathe. His right hand slipped to her hip while his left captured her hand from his shoulder, his fingers lovingly embracing hers. The furrow in his brow melted like the sunset across the horizon and his eyelids lowered while his smoldering gaze flashed bright beneath the fringe of his lashes.

Her body moved like a puppet on a string. Effortlessly, they glided across the dance space her body responding to his touch. The corners of her mouth rose like the sun on a cloudless day and she was on the outside looking in as she watched her body, twirled and turned like a practiced contestant before a panel of judges. Her feet seemed to obey only his commands as he guided her with the slightest of touches across the hard, packed ground.

This was what she remembered, the effortless way their bodies flowed together, swaying as one. An indescribable joy bubbled from a spot buried deep within her soul. Their gazes were no longer locked by a battle of wills, but rather joined in voiceless exploration. If she could put time in a bottle, this was the moment she'd save.

As the last note faded, a furrow rippled across his forehead. Her feet stumbled.

His calloused hands gripped her tighter. The dance and magic faded fast like fireworks in the night sky. The bright, bursting colors turned into wisps of smoke as accusations from the past washed over them. The warmth that had raced through her fluid limbs turned cold.

His commanding body turned to granite. Awkwardly they stood, chest to chest as if they were in grade school, waiting for the next set of dance instructions from the gym teacher.

Another song began, but they remained rooted to the spot. Seconds moved like minutes. Her muscles grew tense, waiting. He needed to make a move, she decided. She wouldn't beg him to listen again. *He* was the one who needed to apologize or to ask why.

Those around them moved to the music. Bumped from behind, she heard a murmured apology and a remark about this being a dance floor.

If Ben heard, he didn't acknowledge the comment. He trembled beneath her hand, his lips parted, she held her breath, waiting, but no words came.

Should I stay or go? Her throat tightened against the words she wanted to say. She needed to know, was this just two people thrown together on a crowded dance floor...or a push of fate?

A minute ago, he was liquid gold flowing beneath her fingertips, but now he was as stiff as the cat Miss Ellen accidentally locked in her trunk for three weeks.

He closed his eyes and his hands dropped to his sides. She stepped back. *I have my answer.* Ben clearly wasn't interested in her. She brushed the pigtails from her shoulders, turned and walked away, chastising herself for straining her ears in his direction. She knew it was foolish, but she hoped he'd call her back.

Pride kept the lump from growing and the tears from coming. She was here to listen to music and enjoy the day. *Although she wished she would have had one last kiss, if Ben didn't want to kiss her, well then maybe the pirate did.* The images numbed the pain and by the time she caught up to Shellie, she forced a slight smile. "I'm ready for a beer. How about you?"

Shellie's complexion had faded from rosy to white and she absently brushed a hand over the bandage on her forehead.

"Are you okay?"

"Fine, just a little tired." Her friend bent to rub her toes. "And these new sandals are killing my feet."

"Wait here then and I'll get us some drinks."

It didn't take long for Alex to find one of the beer booths. After digging her driver's license out of her back pocket, she got into line. She brushed her hand along her shorts, her palm still warm from Ben's body. His brown eyes had been molten; if he would have bent to kiss her, she was certain she would have fainted. She swallowed while her parched lips stuck to her teeth. After all he had put her through his touch should anger her instead—

There came a sudden tap on her shoulder. She whirled around. "Can't you leave me alone?" Her cheeks warmed. "Oops. I thought you were someone else," she apologized into Patrick's startled eyes.

"Well, lucky for me, I'm not the wrong guy. Guess that makes me the right one?" He casually draped an arm over her shoulders. "For the record, Ben's crazy for wanting that hat. Me, I'd give you the moon if I could."

She casually tossed her head, a slight smile on her lips. "So, how good of friends are you and Ben?" Her voice was light and her eyes focused on a spot past Patrick.

"We're on the same softball team."

Disappointed in his answer, she tried to think of another way to pry the information out of him. Clearly, they were friends and he probably could give her some insight into Ben. *Had he really been heartbroken? How tight was he with the redhead?* She shouldn't even care, but she couldn't help herself either. "Play ball together for a long time?"

He reached out and touched a strand of beads. "Mmm-hmm."

She studied his face. His eyes shimmered with amusement as the corner of his mouth twitched. Apparently, she wasn't very clever. "It's not what you think." She captured his hand in hers and brought it away from her chest, but didn't let go as his thumb caressed her skin. "We didn't get them the usual way. Shellie *bought* them." Alex shuffled along in the slow-moving line.

"Do you think she'd notice if one strand was missing?" Patrick-the-pirate moved their hands slowly back toward the beads.

"I'm sure she'll never miss one strand." Alex forced his hands back down to her side.

The pirate took hold of her other hand and placed them both on his waist. Manipulating them beneath his, he had her palms slide his shirt up ever so slowly. When her fingers brushed against naked skin, she ripped her fingers away, shaking them like a stick caught on fire.

Patrick grinned. "So, do I get some beads?"

"*Just* beads," she said firmly, not wanting to give him the wrong impression.

Laughter rumbled from Patrick's chest. He wrapped his arms around her and spun her in a circle. "You're a one-of-a-kind girl there, Alex. A *my* girl, if I ever saw one."

Inches between them, hearts pounding, Alex stuttered, "W-what color do you want?"

Deep and low, his voice teased the soft skin on her neck. "Green, to match your eyes. I'm going to wear them forever and think of you always."

She picked a green strand, but from all the dancing, the beads had gotten tangled.

"Here let me help." Patrick offered.

His gaze swept slowly over the beads, the corners of his mouth split in a wide grin, and he murmured unintelligibly. Alex lightly slapped his hand away from her chest. "No, I'll do it."

He moved a little closer. "You don't trust me." His head tilted and his gaze peered beneath drooping eyelids. "You thought I was going to cop a feel."

She paused with her hands on the beads. She hadn't meant to offend Patrick. "It's just...I..."

He leaned in and placed a kiss on her cheek. "Trust your instincts. There isn't a guy here that doesn't want to put his hands all over you."

She took a step back. There was one...Ben. Her hand paused on the strand of beads.

Fingers trailed up her arms. "Are you sure you don't want some help."

The green strand slid free. "Got them." She held the beads up for the pirate.

"Put them on me." He winked. "Please."

Alex shrugged and held the beads up over his head. Before she could drop them over his bandana, he growled. Startled, she dropped them.

"Aye, Missy." He wrapped his arms around her in a quick hug. "You're so much fun to tease."

They both bent down to retrieve the beads and bumped heads. Laughing in his arms, she finally managed to get the beads over his head. Why couldn't this teaser be the one her heart wanted?

Someone cleared his throat loudly. When Alex turned, the line had moved. "Sorry." She and Patrick giggled and bumped into each other as they moved closer to the front. Before she had a chance to order a beer, a number of men had lined up before her, flashing their chest and bellies. Wide eyed, she glanced at Patrick.

He grinned, leaned in and whispered, "I'd give them beads."

"Would it be okay if I offered some of them two strands *not* to lift up their shirts?"

His laughter once again bubbled forth and he shook his head.

Like a queen knighting her subjects, she quickly handed out the strands.

"Next." The man behind the counter called out.

Patrick's arm slipped around her shoulders as he walked her up to the counter. "Two beers."

"Make it three." Alex reached for her money.

The pirate turned her slightly in his arms. "I don't mind buying you two beers if you're really thirsty, but I don't want to buy a beer for your boyfriend."

She set a twenty on the counter. "I'm buying...and the other one is for Shellie."

Patrick picked up her money and gave it back. "Well then, this is definitely my treat."

"Thank you."

"Believe me, the pleasure has been all mine." His smile was slight, but so bright you wouldn't have been able to miss it.

On their return to find Shellie, the cups of beer sloshed, forcing Alex to stop every couple of steps to take a sip. When they were almost back to the spot where she had left her friend, Alex stopped again. Her beer was half gone and a quarter of Shellie's beer was on the ground.

"So, do you have a boyfriend back home?" Patrick asked.

"No boyfriend." Alex took small steps.

"Don't tell me you've waited a year for Ben?" He stared at her, paused, and then shook his head. "Oh crap. I know that look. You have." Brows fell heavily over his eyes and the corners of his mouth drooped. "What does that guy have that I don't?"

She stopped and her limbs turned to lead. "You're wrong. Maybe at one time I had a *thing* for Ben, but certainly not after this weekend. He's rude, conceited and called me some pretty ugly names." Her feet shuffled forward. "Now help me look for Shellie," she demanded.

"You don't have to bite my head off. If you say there's nothing between you, I believe you." He draped an arm over her shoulder. "Beside, I knew the moment I laid eyes on you, you were too good for the likes of Ben."

She ignored Patrick and scanned the horizon, but instead of finding Shellie, she spied Ben again. Her steps faltered. "Speak of the devil," she mumbled and came to a dead stop.

Patrick bumped her hip and a little more beer spilled.

Alex's gaze focused on the redhead securely clasped to Ben's arm. The two of them laughed, and if they were aware of Patrick and her, they gave no acknowledgement.

"It's too bad you don't have a *thing* for him. I could have helped you get over it."

Patrick gave her a slight squeeze and she stepped out from under his arm. His eyes crinkled— he really did have a wicked smile.

"Tempting," she said, honestly.

He danced in front of her. "Are you telling me I have a chance?"

"We can start as friends and maybe—if you're good—by the end of the weekend I'll give you a little kiss."

He stopped, leaned over the two beers she held and whispered warm against her cheek, "Aye, mate. I think you're succumbing to my charm."

She surprised them both by giving him a peck on the cheek. "Aye."

"Over here," Shellie called out, interrupting the moment.

She laughed and scurried away from Patrick.

Shellie paused as she reached for her beer. "What happened to all my beads?"

Alex glanced at her beadless chest. "I ran into Patrick and he wanted a strand of beads. Next thing

I knew, there was a line of men lifting their shirts." She fluttered her eyelids. "What could I do, but give them their hard-earned prizes?"

"I did start the bead thing." Patrick grinned. "But I'd be happy to replace them."

"You remember Patrick," she said by way of introduction.

Bumped from behind, she sloshed what remained of Shellie's beer over the ground. "Ugh." She tipped her cup upside down grasping the few leftover droplets on her tongue. "I feel like the baby bear in Goldilocks, 'And somebody drank my beer a-a-all up,'" the starlet cried with a dramatic pout.

The pirate laughed. "I want *you* to tell me a bedtime story. I can't wait to hear what happens when the bear finds Goldilocks in his bed after she drank all his beer."

"My, my, what big—," Alex chimed in.

Her friend bumped her shoulder. "No, you got the story wrong. You're thinking of Little Red *Goes Riding*."

Patrick and Alex laughed along with a blushing Shellie.

"Beer here," a vendor called out. He had a keg on his back and a sign boasting fill-ups for six dollars.

"I still owe you a beer."

Alex called the man over to fill up Shellie's cup. Patrick also had his cup refilled and then insisted on paying.

Shellie pointed in the direction of the bull rides. "Want to go watch? It'll be a while before the next act takes the stage."

The pirate casually draped his arm over Alex's shoulder. "*I* could teach you how to ride a bull," he whispered as his finger drew lazy circles on her skin.

She wished her heart raced from his touch and desire course through her veins with the mere thought of his lips touching hers. Then again, the thought of kissing Patrick didn't make her want to throw up either. So, maybe the chemistry would come.

The trio found a spot among the crowd gathering around the mechanical bull. The operator shouted out challenges and pointed to the trophies on display. "To the winner goes the spoils and if that isn't enough, we have T-shirts and individual photos for sale."

"I wish I could ride a bull." Shellie gingerly touched the bandage on her head.

Alex shook hers. "I don't think that'd be wise," she said as the jubilant mood of the crowd washed over her. The sun shone brightly and the smell of fried foods added to the carnival atmosphere.

Behind her, a familiar, high-pitched laugh sent a chill up her spine. She tucked her fingers tight into the crook of Patrick's arm. He looked down and smiled curiously.

The voice attached to the laughter grated on her nerves. When she glanced to her right, Ben was less than fifty feet away. His girlfriend cackled next to him, but his unyielding glare was focused on Alex.

Patrick pulled her chin around.

Her eyes and mouth popped open in surprise.

"I don't mind being used."

Patrick's words tickled her ear.

"As long as you do it right."

His hand no longer cradled her chin as his arms swept around her back, his eyelids lowered. Before she could react, he had her tipped so far back that her foot kicked up to hold their balance. His lips hit their mark noisily.

The air whooshed from Alex's lungs. The move had taken her completely by surprise though the sensation wasn't totally unpleasant. Tipped back with strong arms holding her up and his lips caressing hers, she couldn't help but feel like a leading lady. She murmured her satisfaction, as she played her part.

When both her feet were on solid ground, she gave Patrick a wink and glanced through the audience for one person in particular. Her shoulders quaked. Ben wasn't looking *at* her, he was looking right through her.

Patrick's thumb trailed beneath her chin and he brought her attention back to him. "It's more effective if you aren't so obvious."

She gave the pirate a good nature thump on the chest then her eyes narrowed as she recalled their first meeting, and Patrick's cryptic words—had the pirate known all along Ben would reject her?

Chapter Eleven

Ben couldn't believe Patrick was moving in on Alex. His stomach constricted. He couldn't believe Patrick was *kissing* her.

He took a step in their direction, but Julia squeezed his arm, momentarily halting his steps and thoughts. Wait, what was he thinking anyway? One minute he couldn't get far enough away from Alex, and the next, he wanted to hold her in his arms and never let her go. She had his thoughts spinning faster than a tornado cutting a path of destruction, uprooting and scattering his judgment.

Scattered or not, the one thing he did know was that he didn't want Patrick anywhere near her.

While he pretended to listen to Julia, his mind stayed on Alex. Something didn't add up. When they danced, everything clicked, from the way their bodies fit together to the easy way they fell into step with each other.

He pushed aside the memory of the dance and watched with wry amusement as Patrick tried to hold her attention. No matter what his so-called friend did, though, every couple of minutes Alex would turn like a child at church, more interested in what was going on behind her than in front of her. His spirits lifted. Maybe she wasn't as cool as she pretended to be. Which please him. Why? He scratched his head. Did he still want her?

He jammed his hand into his pocket. *Doesn't matter.* It wasn't the whole hat thing that bugged him now, but Julia's play-by-play of the conversation in the bathroom that twisted his insides. Alex wasn't out to find him. She wasn't even out to find the best man. From what Julia said, Alex was looking for all the things that love *couldn't* buy. He pulled his hand from his pocket and scratched his scalp. But that didn't make sense either. Patrick was neither rich nor pretentious.

He put the cup with the ice-cold brew to his lips. *Is she trying to make me jealous?* His heart fell to his feet. *Is all this just for show...or is she really falling for Patrick?*

He brought the cup down and ran the back of his hand across his mouth.

"Hey, cowboy, you're a million miles away." Julia took his beer and guzzled what was left before tossing the empty cup to the ground. "And I don't like that the trip is with the bitch twenty feet away."

His gaze lingered only a moment more on Alex before turning to Julia. "That potty mouth of yours is getting old."

Julia's arms wrapped tightly around him. "Give me time, cowboy, and I can make you forget what's her name."

He draped his arm loosely across her back, but she didn't fit in his arms the way Alex had.

Julia shifted her weight from foot to foot. "Damn, that beer is going right through me." She grabbed his head, pulled him close and plastered a quick kiss on his lips before dancing toward the port-a-potties.

Ben resisted the urge to run the back of his hand across his mouth a second time. He walked over to the beer vendor and got another pint. Hopefully, Julia wouldn't feel obligated to drink this beer, too. His intentions were to stand around and wait for her, but his body had a mind of its own as his feet fluently strode over to Alex. Like an insect bite, he couldn't leave her alone. He knew he shouldn't scratch, yet the desire was greater than the control. He had no idea what he'd say or what he hoped to accomplish, but something in him couldn't stand there and watch Patrick sweet-talk Alex.

His friend looked up first. "Hey, Benny-boy. What can I do for you?"

He grinned and pushed his cup into his buddy's hand. "You can hold my beer, while I kiss your girlfriend."

In one movement, he stepped in front of Alex and lowered his lips to hers. The kiss was no more than a whisper and a promise as his mouth brushed against her parted lips, yet his heart hammered to a beat that was no longer in step with his mind. His head screamed for him to turn around, but his hands picked up the rhythm of his heart and rose to hold her face closer. The skin on her shoulders slid beneath his hands like silk and she smelled like a summer breeze, warm and fragrant. His arms trembled as he resisted the urge to crush her to his chest. His lips tingled from the sweetness of her mouth and the need of wanting her, despite everything. His heart pounded as it tried to get closer to hers.

Her resistance melted and she slid closer to him. He trailed kisses along her jaw line and thrilled to the murmur that escaped her lips. His lips brushed her earlobe. "I would have given you the hat."

In an instant her body went from warm and inviting, to hard and cold. Her palms slapped his chest as her back arched. She staggered backwards, the dreamy expression in her eyes engulfed by flames.

"I don't want your stupid hat, or your kisses," she spat.

Her words said one thing, but her body quite another. *Damn.* He had no doubt if he hadn't opened his mouth she'd still be in his arms. A grin tickled his lips; she sure was a spitfire. His fingers brushed her forearm. "That came out wrong."

Time ticked slowly as their eyes locked. He searched for a line that would make things right. "If I told you you were beautiful would you hold it against me?"

Hands clenched into fists at her sides, a vein pulsing in her neck, she said, "If you were the last man..."

Her eyes were cold and her lips were drawn tighter than Mrs. Riley's purse strings when her old man asked for beer money. He chuckled hoping to lighten the mood. "It was just a kiss—"

"*And it was just a hat*, but that didn't seem to stop you from calling me names."

They stood nose to nose, and their chests rose and fell in quick succession.

"I told you the hat was for my brother." He tried to hold his temper, to explain as his hand brushed her shoulder.

She flinched at the brief contact.

His thoughts spun in one direction, his heart in another. He wanted to pull close and kiss her until they were beyond thinking. He didn't want to walk away, not yet. He wanted to give her the chance to explain, *hoping* that he had been rash...and not right.

She staggered back a step. "Like that's suppose to mean something to me? So he lost a hat and was a little disappointed. I'm sure he got over it." Her voice grew in volume. "Do you have any idea what *I* lost?"

Her words hit him like bricks.

Her left hand slapped flat against his chest, her right balled into a fist. "No, you don't because you are the most pig-headed, self-centered man around. You wouldn't even let me explain."

"I'm here now, and I'm listening."

Alex glared at him. "You had your chance."

Her voice lost its volume and a chill went down his spine at the whispered words. He could handle her anger, but the thought of her indifference sucked the air from his lungs.

"More than once," she added pointedly. "Now it's too late."

"Hey, man," Patrick interrupted. "Might be best if you took a walk."

Ben took a step and stopped. He didn't want to leave like this. If he walked away from her now, he knew he'd be making a mistake.

Arms crossed tightly under her chest, she didn't look at him, but through him.

"I'm...I just..." His chest grew tight at the hurt on her face. He'd been an idiot, he saw that now in the wounded green eyes. Suddenly, the only important thing was what Alex thought, not what everyone else did. Indecision at how to make things right caused him to stagger forward. "Alex, I—"

"Leave me alone," she said, her voice flat as she turned from him.

Patrick grabbed Ben's hand before he could reach Alex.

"Go," Patrick mouthed.

Ben glared and wanted nothing more than to shove his friend away from Alex. His stomach clenched as Patrick draped his arm across Alex's shoulders. He stood slacked jawed as he watched his friend lead her away.

Watching them walk away was the hardest thing he had ever done. He had the distinct feeling he'd just blown it...again. A boulder of emotion slid down his throat and threatened to crush his heart.

Ben slapped his thigh out of frustration as his boots kicked up dirt. A man in a black leather vest, jeans and a matching hat stepped in front of him before he could leave. Ben scowled and took a step to the right. The man moved and blocked Ben's way.

He would have loved to bowl the man over, but instead stopped, his voice reflecting his frustration. "Excuse me."

"Hold up, cowboy." The guy grabbed his arm. "I'm Darlin' Dan, the emcee of the festival and K2010's disc jockey."

"Whatever you're selling, I'm not interested." Ben pushed his hand away.

"Not selling a thing. In fact, I'd like to offer you five thousand dollars—"

Ben eyed the DJ up and down. "What's the catch?"

"You look like you could've been on a bull or two and I'm in need of some riders for a charity bull riding contest for couples. You win and you choose where the money is donated—"

"I don't have a partner." He took a step to the right, only to have the man sidestep with him.

"The partner's not a problem. We'll take care of that. I just need the manpower and I'm sure a charity of your choice could use the money. I'll even toss in VIP tickets to next year's concert."

Ben stopped—not for the tickets, but because of his brother. Five thousand dollars could really help the special needs camp Dustin attended. Besides, he could use the physical outlet to release some of his pent-up emotions. Alex made it clear she wanted nothing to do with him, and Julia was grating on his nerves. Ben nodded crisply and the DJ slapped him on the shoulder.

"I just need you to sign a consent form and pick up a number." He pointed him in the direction of a table set up under a canopy.

While Ben stood in line assessing his competition, his mood lightened. This might be the first smart thing he had done all weekend. He'd ridden before and had a chance at winning the prize. It would be nice to be able to give a little something back to Camp Special Needs; they'd been great with his brother.

"Next." The man slid a paper and pen at Ben. He glanced quickly over the forms then signed his name and went outside the tent to wait for the next set of instructions. His heart stopped as he spied Alex and Patrick headed to the table. They signed up, the last two.

"Hey, cowboy, are you going to ride?"

Ben spun around. Focused on the other couples, he didn't hear Julia slip up behind him. "Yeah, I guess."

"Me, too," she drawled, her voice throaty.

Darlin' Dan stopped any further conversation. "Okay, we have everyone paired up. When we call your names come to the table and get your numbers."

Over Julia's shoulder, he watched Patrick slip his arm around Alex. He cringed, but like witnessing a car wreck, he stopped and gawked.

"Cowboy," Julia whispered. "I hoped you'd ride with me."

The deep voice called out the first couple. "Julia Shartan and Patrick Hughes come get your number."

Julia presented a pout. "I wanted you."

He brushed his hand across his upper lip to hide the grin breaking his face. "Don't worry. With Patrick, it will only be a two second ride."

"Well, I hope *you* will be able to improve upon his time later tonight." Her voice was sultry as she left to join her team-mate.

A chill went through him. He'd prefer bedding down in a patch of prickly ash. He rolled his eyes as Julia's hips swayed. She walked by the table, picked up the numbers and descended on Patrick and Alex like a vulture. Ben wasn't sure what was going on but from the expression on Alex's face, he was certain the exchange between the two girls was anything but friendly.

If he wasn't so annoyed at Patrick he might have gone over and helped him out of the sticky situation. But, as it was, Ben was content to watch Patrick struggle to keep Alex at arm's length while Julia used his teammate's body for a shield.

They called out a couple more names. Patrick circled slowly as did the two women.

"Alexandra Ellen Coe," the announcer shouted again.

Patrick turned Alex around, pointed her in the direction of the table and gave her a firm push. She stumbled forward, paused and gave a withering glance behind her.

Ben was glad he wasn't in Julia's shoes.

So that's who she was, *Alexandra Ellen Coe*. He smiled. The name reminded him of David Allan Coe, who wrote *The Perfect Country and Western Song*. Next to anything by Toby Keith, *The Perfect Country and Western Song* was his brother's favorite. Maybe it was another small sign that he'd done the right thing by signing up for this bull ride.

"Ben Buck?"

Definitely a sign. His luck must be changing.

He headed to the table. Alex's eyes darted about until they landed on him...and her face drained of color. He rushed forward, fearing she was going to faint.

Quite the opposite. She stepped back up to the table and slapped her palms down. "I can't be partners with that man. Draw another name!"

Chapter Twelve

The man shook his head and handed Alex the numbers. "No can do."

"*Please.*"

He glanced from Ben to Alex. "Why?"

The numbers fluttered to the ground as her hands landed on her hips. "It's a long story."

"Chances are, you won't be together for more than eight seconds anyways," he snickered. "If you'll excuse me." He turned his back and headed through the crowd to the center of the tent.

Ben bent down and picked up the numbers. "I'm not happy about this either," he said, not even attempting to hide his grin.

"Yes, you are. You probably paid the guy off just so you and your girlfriend could torture me." Green eyes sparked as white teeth flashed.

"Gather round," Darlin' Dan shouted. "As soon as everyone has their numbers pinned to the back of their shirts, we'll draw numbers to see what order you ride in...and then we'll get started."

Ben was certain Alex didn't hear a word the man said as she stood, hands across her chest, eyes glaring at him. *Alexandra Ellen Coe.* He rolled the name over in his mind, certain he had heard the name somewhere before.

His gaze caught on a heart-shaped tattoo on her arm. *She didn't have that last year.* The *Mother* inside puzzled him even more.

"If you're done staring, you can give me my number now."

He smiled. At least she was no longer indifferent. He cocked an eyebrow. "So, you're going to ride with me?"

"I don't see that I have a choice. I can't win the VIP passes if I don't ride." Her fingers brushed across his hand, her eyes large as she yanked a number from his grip.

Ben held in a chuckle; she was a horrible actress. His presence affected her...she was attracted to him and it made her angry. Why?

His voice a mere caress. "You plan to come back next year, then?" he asked in a voice he hoped was as smooth as a caress.

Her eyes rolled.

The emcee's voice rang out, "Does everyone have their numbers pinned on?"

"Can you help?" Ben asked, handing the number and safety pin to Alex. He turned, and waited for the stab in the back. But, instead of a poke, her hand was warm across his back.

"Done," she said with a slight tremor.

He let out a slow breath, grateful she didn't take advantage of the moment to wound him.

She handed her matching number over and presented her back. He grinned as her muscles twitched beneath his hand. Through the checkered material, he could feel her heart pound. *She wasn't as cool as she pretended to be.* She wasn't even breathing.

He wondered if he slid his hand down to the small of her back and brushed his lips against the pulse in her neck if she'd resist him. He swallowed, surprised at how much he wanted to do just that. This might be his last chance.

"Anytime now," she huffed.

"Don't want it to be crooked. I know how you ladies like everything perfect." His hand moved slowly, not wanting to rush, both literally and

143

figuratively. He needed to be certain before he risked his heart a second time.

Her hand reached around. "I'll do it—"

"Settle down." He watched her lungs work overtime and felt the rapid pulse of her heart beneath his hands. The corners of his mouth tipped wider. He stirred her emotions, and for now, he'd be content with that.

"If you're having trouble, I'm sure I can find someone to help," she said impatiently.

"Just taking my time. Wouldn't want to stick you with a pin now, would I?" he whispered into her ear.

His hand slid down her back.

Her foot stomped and she lowered her voice. "Don't get any ideas."

Too late. He already had plenty of ideas and not one included riding a bull. He stepped back, trying to get the images of her out of his head and the taste of her kiss off his tongue. No such luck. Following her into the line, he watched her pick a number from Darlin' Dan's black hat.

"Twenty. You'll be the last couple to compete," the announcer told them as he wrote their numbers and names on a roster.

"Hey, what number did you draw?" Patrick asked as he steered Julia away from Alex.

Ben glanced at Alex, coiled as tight as a rattlesnake and just as dangerous. Her eyes focused on Julia. He searched his pocket for a stick of gum. Had he read Alex wrong, was she jealous of Julia being with Patrick?

Julia moved to the far side of Ben and clutched his arm. "Miss me?"

Alex moved toward Patrick, her grim gaze never leaving Julia.

"So, what number did you draw?" Patrick asked again.

"Twenty. What did you get?" Ben's eyes focused on the two ladies. The way they were glaring daggers at each other, he figured it was only a matter of time before someone decided to sharpen their claws. He caught Patrick's attention and nodded toward the women.

His friend raised his eyebrows and flapped his jaw, but no sound came out. Ben smirked, thinking Patrick was doing a replay of the last time the women met.

Alex gave Patrick a shove and the smirk on his face disappeared.

"We're number seventeen." His arms went around her as he attempted to cajole her back. "Come on—"

She slid out from underneath his arm. "I think I'll wait with Shellie."

Ben stopped chewing his gum. He watched Alex make her way over to the spot where her friend stood. The only thing he could think about was holding Alex and the thought that she'd be wedged between his legs made it that much better. He wouldn't be holding on to win, he wanted her in his arms one last time and this time he prayed he wouldn't say anything stupid.

His friends sauntered over. Mike had a grin that wouldn't stop and Laurie's' eyes were only partially opened—only too obvious what had delayed those two.

"What's with the numbers?" He poked Patrick on the back.

Julia laughed. "The pirate and I are getting into the saddle together."

"No!" Laurie brushed the blond curls from her eyes. She glanced from Ben to Patrick and back again.

"Yep." Julia moved closer to Laurie, and the two of them stepped off to the side.

"So why are you two doing this?" Mike asked.

Patrick smirked. "Anytime I can crawl into the saddle with a woman..."

Ben pulled another stick of gum from his shirt pocket and popped it into his mouth. "And I was thinking how I'd like to win that money for Dustin's summer camp—"

Patrick punched his arm. "Who are you kidding? By the way you were looking at Alex, it isn't charity you have your mind. The thought of wrapping my arms and legs around her was the only thing that got me to sign on the dotted line."

Ben's stomach clenched around a bellyful of fire. He gave Patrick a shove and resisted the urge to knock him to the ground. "You owe me a beer. I asked you to hold mine earlier, not drink it."

"*You* owe *me*." Patrick's arms shot up into the air. "Alex and I were connecting and then you come along and pull a stunt like that. I can't believe you actually stole a song title." He got right up into Ben's face. "Hold my beer, while I kiss your girlfriend? Ha!"

Mike's hand grasped his shoulder and momentarily blocked his view of Patrick. "I'm sure I only heard half the story, but from the way you've been acting lately, I'm inclined to believe Patrick. Buy him a beer, and me, too," Mike added.

Ben grinned. The kiss had been worth it—in more ways then one. "Okay, I'll buy the beer." He glanced at the bull ride and saw that the first couple hadn't even gotten on yet. "This contest is going to take awhile. The least one of you could do is help me carry the drinks."

Patrick pointed to the spot where Alex and her friend stood. "I'll go keep the girls company."

In less than ten minutes, Ben and Mike were back with the drinks.

"Thanks." Laurie said as Mike turned toward

her and Julia, sloshing beer from his three plastic cups.

"You're welcome," Ben replied as he stepped carefully around them and carried the cardboard tray holding four more cups toward Alex. She wasn't smiling, but she wasn't turning away either. He gave her his best smile, which wasn't hard to do; she was rather adorable in pigtails.

After the plastic cups were passed out, Ben said, "I propose a toast, to winning."

"No, no," Shellie said, before they could clink glasses. "You can't toast to winning, because two of you have to lose. I say we toast to...happy endings."

Alex tipped her head in Ben's direction. Her cheeks went from dusty pink to a strawberry flush.

Ben held up his glass. "Happy endings." He tapped the plastic brim first to Alex's glass then Shellie's.

Patrick held his glass up. "To you, Benny-boy. It's happy trails. I think your little woman Julia is waving you in." He squinted. "Or she's doing an imitation of a helicopter."

Ben turned. Julia's arms flapped so fast and hard that it was possible she'd take off. Ben grinned at the thought and turned his attention back to Alex. "Ever ridden before?"

"Cowboy! Cowboy," Julia shouted out in a sing-song way.

Ben shook his head. "I'll be back."

"*Happy trails to you...*" Patrick sang as Ben shuffled over to Julia.

"Cowboy," she purred, wrapping her arms around him. "I don't like it when you're with that bitch. She's playing you like a fool. She comes around and you're like a Bassett hound, stepping all over yourself just to get close. It's embarrassing."

His gaze narrowed. "Hey, I'm sorry that this weekend hasn't been what—"

"If you're sorry, you'll let me have the hat. If I were wearing it, she'd know it was over, that you were through."

"Not happening." He nodded in the direction of the tent and corral where the mechanical bull was set up. "I'm going to step over and watch the riders. If you don't want to come with me, I'll understand," he added, hoping she'd get the hint. He moved closer to the contestants. His heart sank when Julia followed.

He kept some space between them and pretended he didn't hear half her questions, which was easy to do with the crowd cheering and chanting. So far, nobody had stayed on more than a couple of seconds.

Julia poked him in the side, her lip curled. "Two can play this game." A bright big smile came onto her face. Her hand waved frantically. "Hey, Patrick," Julia called out.

Ben rolled his eyes. *Drama.* His thoughts flew from his mind like the couples who let go of the bull. His attention was drawn to Alex as she warily walked a step behind Patrick.

Julia rushed Patrick, plastering her chest against him. "So, pirate. You know anything about staying in the saddle."

He chuckled and tossed his arm around her. "Come on."

Ben watched Patrick guide Julia to the rail. No doubt, his friend was going to try to give her instructions on how to sit on a saddle. He tried to relax as Alex leaned on the railing next to him.

Clearly, the majority of the contestants had never done this before and the one guy that looked like he might have had some experience was paired up with a woman who looked like she sat on nothing but Italian leather. Surely, there was no way she'd risk breaking a nail just to stay on the bull?

148

He was right. The couple didn't even make it three seconds. The guy swooped down and scooped the woman up off the padded platform. Their kiss lasted longer than their bull ride, leaving the crowd whooping and hollering in encouragement.

Why couldn't he find a woman like that, all warm and loving, willing to take a risk?

From the man's Skoal ring, to their tan lines and boots, it was obvious the next couple had spent some time working outdoors. This woman mounted the bull like she had done it a time or two as well.

"I think we have some competition," Ben said. "You just might be buying tickets next year."

Alex shrugged. "Why?"

He tipped his head, and tried to make eye contact. "Have you ever ridden a bull? Or even a horse?"

She looked down at his boots. "No."

He scratched his head. Why wouldn't she look at him? Was she afraid of what he'd see if he gazed into her eyes? "Well, that woman has."

"And I suppose you're a real cowboy." Her eyes finally came up to meet his stare head on.

"I've certainly spent my fair share in the saddle."

She made a big production of looking him up and down. His mouth split into a teeth-flashing smile. *She still has a thing for me.* He flexed his muscles and turned slowly around. "Some say this is my best side." He presented her with his behind.

"Lot of time in the saddle, huh?" She chuckled as her eyes sparkled mischievously. "Let me guess...you're a carnival worker in charge of the merry-go-round."

He took it as a good sign that she was relaxing— he could lose himself in her eyes. "Actually, I work the family farm. We supply horses to the YMCA and Girl Scout summer camps."

Her smile turned warm and inviting. Ben wondered if he'd be rushing things if he leaned in and stole a kiss. His fingers reached out and brushed a pigtail from her shoulder.

A loud cheer went up and they both turned toward the arena.

He glanced at the clock that displayed the couples' time. "Wow."

"Eighteen seconds, is that good?" Alex asked.

She was so close, it would be so easy to lean in and brush his lips across her cheek. He resisted, not wanting to take the chance of having the humor in her eyes extinguished. "Yeah, going to be hard to beat."

Darlin' Dan made a big production out of the couple's time. "It'll be tough for the remaining contestants. Eighteen seconds, the new official time to beat!"

Patrick walked over with Julia. "Did you see that? They're nothing but a bunch of showoffs. Ringers brought in I bet!"

Julia moved in next to Ben. "You'd better be careful. If that pirate is half as good in the saddle as he claims to be, you're going to have some competition, cowboy." She practically purred as her hands moved up and down Ben's chest. When she started to rub against him, he pushed her aside and held her an arms length away.

"Want to make a little wager that I can stay in the saddle longer than you?" Patrick suggested. "Two seconds my—"

"Hey." Ben dropped Julia's hands. "There are ladies present."

Alex turned toward Patrick. "It isn't worth the bother. Besides, everyone knows it's the woman who controls the ride."

"That's right," Julia sputtered towards Alex. "And I can keep my man in the saddle longer than you can. You're nothing but a polished tease. Me, I'm the real thing."

"Puleeze." Alex stepped closer. "You're probably not even a redhead and the only thing you're accomplished at is lying in a vertical position."

Julia's arms started in motion. "I am too a redhead." She rushed toward Alex with her nails clawed.

Ben scooped up Julia, arms flaying and legs kicking.

"She can't talk to me that way. I'll show that tramp how to ride. Put me down!"

Ben set her down on the other side of Patrick who immediately wrapped an arm around Julia's waist.

"Come on there, Red. Let's show them how it's done."

"You might want to take notes," she sputtered. "I'm going to show you how a *real* woman does it."

Alex's eyes rolled as her fingers fluttered a goodbye. "Whatever."

Ben's smile widened. A win-win situation. Not only was Julia no longer hanging on him, but with Patrick out of the picture, he had Alex to himself. Bummer was, there she stood, preoccupied and looking at anything but him.

Finally, he gave up and settled for standing so close that his arms continually brushed up against hers. He gave her a little nudge and arched his eyebrow.

Alex rolled her eyes but didn't move. *Promising.*

Patrick and Julia had entered the bullpen.

The pirate was theatrical, walking like a sea captain after a long voyage. "Aye, nothing to it, sweetheart. I hear it's no different than staying on deck during a hurricane or hopping into bed with a real wench."

Julia's laughter rang out a split second before

the crowd's. Her arms wrapped around him. "You ain't experienced nothing till you've climbed in the saddle with me."

The crowd cheered.

"All right," Darlin' Dan announced. "Let's see if this lovely couple can work the bull as well as the crowd."

Patrick easily picked up Julia and set her on the well-worn back of the metal bull. He showed her how to curl her hand through the attached handle and climbed on behind her.

He incited the fans into more laughter as his hand landed on Julia's chest. "Just looking for something to hold on to..."

The operator of the mechanical bull sat at a table outside the corral and manipulated the movements of the bull with a swivel stick shift and electronics board. Darlin' Dan sat next to him. The emcee gave a nod and the operator set the bull into motion, slowly spinning to the right.

Julia screamed. The hairs on the back of Ben's neck stood straight up. Patrick couldn't have looked prouder.

The bull rocked back and forth. Julia whooped and hollered. Ben checked the clock, eight seconds. "Not bad."

"Faster! Faster," the crowd chanted.

The operator spun them hard to the right, to the left, to the right, and then quickly lowered the front end of the bull and the two went tumbling over.

Julia squealed.

"Oh, baby!" Patrick wrapped his arms around her and rolled across the soft mat.

The crowd roared their approval as the pirate stole a kiss from his redheaded wench.

"Four seconds short," Darlin' Dan yelled. "But let's give them a hand." After a few seconds when neither got off the ground, he added, "All right, you two. I've got a bucket of cold water here and ain't afraid to use it."

Patrick helped Julia to her feet then raised her hand high in the air to more cheering.

Julia glared at Alex. "Beat that, if you can."

Alex leaned closer to Ben. "Think we can do better?"

Her fresh scent beckoned to him. "Hell, yeah." He wrapped his arms around Alex and dipped her back. The moment their lips met, his arm was yanked from behind.

"Cowboy, that's not what I meant," a pissed-off Julia sneered.

Patrick's voice echoed. "Knock it off."

Alex struggled upright and her gaze darted about. He eased back to give her space after his impulsive action. She stood like a statue, watching the next two couples whose times didn't even come close to the record.

"All right, folks, let's have a nice round of applause for our last couple..."

The pounding of his heart and the rumbling of his stomach drowned out the emcee's voice. It wasn't the ride that was making him nervous, but the thought of Alex wedged between his legs that made his head buzz.

His hand rested on the small of her stiff back. He tried to remove his tongue from the roof of his mouth as they walked across the mat to the bull.

The crowd clapped and hooted.

Alex waved, nervously.

He nodded and stood next to the bull. His hand slid up her waist to help her mount, but she brushed his help aside. She placed her hands on the bull, swung a long, lean leg over and propelled herself onto its back.

His eyebrows rose. "Have you done this before?"

She gave a non-committal shrug.

He climbed up behind her. Just as he figured, her rear end fit snuggly between his legs as her wild, sweet scent filled his lungs. He wasn't sure if it was her body or his that trembled.

Ben pulled her closer. "You don't have to be afraid."

Her body stiffened.

"Relax. The trick is to hold on to the bull with your thighs. You have to squeeze your legs and don't fight the motion, roll with it." His hands cupped the swell of her hips, the material grazing his palms as she shifted.

"Y-you've done this before?" she asked quietly.

Out of the corner of his eye, he saw the emcee nod and the operator put the mechanics in motion before Ben could answer. They rocked forward and his hand gripped her hips. He leaned back and pulled Alex with him. "Don't fight it." His hands slid around to her pelvis and she leaned into him. He moaned.

"Squeeze."

They came up and swung to the left. Alex slipped.

"I've got you," he breathed.

His hands skated to her waist. His fingers ached as they brushed her soft skin beneath her shirt. He wrapped his arms around her, fitting perfectly under the swell of her breasts.

They swung to the left again.

Her heart pounded so hard her back vibrated against his chest. Alex slid sideways again and he tightened her hot body back against him. Prepared to be tossed forward again, this time Alex anticipated the move and pushed her backside tight against him. They were able to stay on. His hands dropped to grip her quivering thighs. He worked as hard to breathe as he did to keep them on the ride.

"Faster! *Faster,*" the crowd cheered frantically.

They swung to the right, tipped forward and swung to the left. Alex ground against his chest. The back of her denim rubbed against him. Like a match against a stone, the spark caught hold and his body burned with desire. Visions erupted in his mind of her body pressed against his in a field of wildflowers, her head in the crook of his arm as they lay beneath the stars, her lips warm and willing on his body, his name on her lips...

Back to a startling reality, he suddenly realized they were too far to the right. His thighs automatically gripped tighter, struggling to get centered. They tipped forward and his weight bore down on Alex.

Crap! The beast tipped in the opposite direction and his thighs lost their grip. Alex strained against his arms, but she couldn't hang on. He sailed backwards, plucking her from the bull, like an eagle snatching a fish from a stream.

His back hit the mat hard, breaking the fall for Alex. Ben welcomed her weight even as the air whooshed from his lungs. On a heavy breath, he pulled her tight, unwilling to let her go.

A collective, "Ahhh," came from the crowd.

Her heart slammed against his arms, and her body trembled. After a moment, she pushed up, the back of her head brushing across his lips as she turned toward the clock.

Her head quickly spun back. "That was only 12 seconds." Her jaw clenched and her gaze turned steely.

He stood, reached for her hand and pulled her up close against him. His thumb and finger brushed across her cheek as he tried to coax a smile from her.

She finally glanced his way and his heart swelled. *Damn, she's beautiful.* "It was the best 12 seconds of my life," he said louder than he'd meant to.

The crowd laughed.

He cringed.

Alex's body stiffened and she struggled against his hold. She headed across the mat toward the exit. He reached for her hand, but she pulled it away. Did winning mean that much to her?

She turned suddenly and shoved him, hard. Her eyes were cold and hard. "You let go on purpose. You wanted *her* to win," she accused, hiking a thumb toward Julia.

"No, I didn't. I wanted *us* to win."

"I don't believe you. Leave me alone."

She hustled toward her friend, but he easily caught up. His fingers brushed against her forearm. "With you in my arms, I got distracted. It wasn't that I wanted them to win, it's that I couldn't think of anything but your—"

She suddenly stopped, turned, and slapped her hands to his chest.

"I'm not a tease *or* a thief. I'm tired of you calling me that."

Her friend gave him an icy glare and took a boxer's stance.

Alex stepped next to her. "Don't bother, Shellie."

Ben shook his head. "No wai—"

She took another step. "Why? I've already wasted a year," she hissed, turned and ran.

Shellie shook her fist. "Stay away," she shouted and jogged after Alex.

Before Ben could run after her, Julia latched onto his arm. Her nails pierced his wrist and anchored him to the spot.

"Don't leave me, cowboy," she begged.

"Julia, let go. I'm not in the mood." He pried her fingers from his arm and walked away.

Things were all mixed up...on both ends. His head spun. *Alexandra Coe.* He turned the name over in his mind as he started in the opposite direction.

In the distance, he heard the whistle from the approaching train and he stopped cold.

That was it—the white cross at the railroad crossing near Kakato Township. *In loving memory of Ellen Coe* was hand written across the small wooden memorial.

He had just gotten back from Country Time last year when he first noticed it. He had stopped into Millie's for coffee and everyone was upset. There had been a number of accidents over the years, but this was the first time anyone had lost their life.

Oh my God. What if that was one of Alex's relatives? His arms fell across his churning stomach. What if she didn't desert him last year?

Maybe she *had* to leave. Could that be why she disappeared so suddenly? And she came back this year...with the hat. *His* hat.

His hands washed over his face before his fingertips applied pressure to his temples. He'd been so mad the moment he saw her with it that he never thought twice, never imagined something so horrible.

What have I done?

Chapter Thirteen

"Hey, wait up."

Alex heard Patrick's voice but kept walking.

"Hey," Shellie brushed her arm. "It's the pirate. Aren't you going to stop?"

"No."

Her friend clamped onto her arm and brought her to a halt. "He's not the one you're mad at. Besides, I'm not going to let Ben ruin your weekend. We're going to have fun, remember?"

She forced half a smile into her granite features. "Yeah."

It was so unfair that with only a touch, Ben could have her wishing and wanting things to be different. When their eyes met, she swore he was sorry and wanted to make amends. But then he brought up the stupid hat, or he rubbed Julia in her face. She clenched her hands as her heart plummeted to the bottom of her feet. *How could I have been so wrong about him?*

Patrick jogged up and slid one arm around Shellie and the other around her. "How's my girls?"

"Great," starlet answered in a peppy singsong.

Alex stiffened. "Fine."

"Ri-i-ght," he murmured, with a doubtful brow.

Patrick turned them around, herding them in the direction they had just come from. Alex dug her heels in. "I'm not going back there."

He squeezed her shoulders. "Okay, but I wasn't going—"

"I don't like your friends." Her feet stopped.

158

Patrick and Shellie skidded to a stop as well. Her hand flayed to the left, and if the Pirate hadn't ducked and stagger-stepped he'd have been sporting a black eye. She forced the words out through a clench jaw. "Every time I see Ben, he brings up the hat. The hat I *returned*. The hat I have yet to even see him wear! He tells me *I'm* a tease when he has Julia dangling from his arm. If he's going to call anyone a tease it would—"

Patrick's laughter rumbled. "Damn, you're sexy when you're mad." He leaned in and planted a kiss on her lips.

She shoved him away. "Knock it off."

The pirate stepped closer to Shellie. "Is she always such a sore loser?"

Alex's hands flew to her hips. "*Loser?* It wasn't *my* fault. Ben's the one that let go. I bet he did it on purpose so you and his little girlfriend could win."

"I don't think—"

She slapped her hands to her ears. "I don't want to hear it. You guys always stick up for each other."

Patrick tugged her hands down. "I've got a great idea. Let's go get some beads." He looped an arm around Alex and Shellie's waists. "Although necklaces will only distract from your beauty."

"I'm beginning to like you." Shellie smiled then shook her fist. "Even though your friend is despicable."

He gave Shellie a little hip check. "I like you ladies, too."

Shellie returned the bump with a little too much hip, staggering Patrick into Alex.

The pent-up anger and tension eased from her shoulders with the comical duo swaying and knocking into each other. When they jumped around doing some crazy dance moves, she couldn't hang onto the frown any longer.

"Come on," Patrick draped his arms around Alex

again. "Let's go get some loot."

Alex grinned wide. "You're buying."

"For you gals, I'd privateer a whole jewelry store."

"Too bad there's none in sight," Shellie said with a giggle.

"If you settle for trinkets today, I'll promise you great treasures tomorrow."

They jockeyed over to the storefronts displaying beads. The little shop was crowded with people purchasing souvenirs and inquiring about disposable rain ponchos.

Alex peeked her head outside and looked up at the sky. *When had the dark, threatening clouds rolled in?* It would only be a matter of minutes before the sun was totally blotted out.

A giggling Girl Scout interrupted her sky watch, followed by Patrick with two necklaces that had beads the size of baseballs—one bright pink and the other a deep purple.

Alex shook her head. "I've never seen balls—beads that big."

Shellie laughed as he placed the hot pink one over her head.

The pirate slipped the heavy necklace over Alex's. "Nice b-b-b-balls." His finger brushed over her tattoo as he released them and she took comfort in his touch. His hand moved down her arm and a shiver went through her.

"You're cold."

"And soon to be wet," Shellie added, pointing up. "We should have brought jackets and an umbrella."

"We've got time between shows," Alex offered. "We could easily run back to the tent, grab gear and get back here before the next performance."

Patrick slinked closer. His voice was warm on her neck. "Perhaps I should walk you two ladies back—" He stopped suddenly. "Whoa."

Alex's next step was halted by a brush of denim against her thigh. An immediate chain reaction occurred—hips, then breast slammed into hard contours and her skin tingled. But, instead of stepping back, her body leaned in closer. She didn't have to look up to see the amused expression in his deep brown eyes or the curve of his sexy lips to know she'd inadvertently slammed into Ben.

"Hey, Mike, Ben," Patrick greeted. "It was nice of you to run into us."

Ben's hand brushed up against her tattoo. Alex jumped back, out of his reach. His hand rose to run through his hair. Her stomach clenched. Once again, he taunted her with his hatless head. Her mind fumed, while her body ached for another touch.

Patrick's head swiveled around the men. "What did you do with the little ladies?"

Mike's eyebrow narrowed. "You ought to know. After the watermelon crawl, they crawled into the tent for a nap."

"Where are you headed to?" Ben asked.

He'd directed the question to her, but Alex held her mouth shut tight.

Patrick smirked. "I was just going to take these lovely women back to their tent and grab a jacket for myself."

"Let Laurie and Julia knows where we are, okay?" Mike asked.

The pirate nodded. "Can do."

Ben's finger brushed the beads on Alex's chest. "You looked much better in my hat—"

She slapped his chest. "Why is it always the damned hat? I didn't steal it." She shoved Ben. "Leave me alone, and tell your girlfriend, too. Or the next time you or your girlfriend get in my way, I'm going to enjoy knocking you down."

Alex stormed away. Muffled in the thunderous rush of blood in her ears, she heard the pirate and the Girl Scout fall into step behind her. They hadn't gone far when she couldn't hold her frustration in any longer. "I don't get it. All that fuss about his stupid hat and he doesn't even wear it."

Patrick winked. "I think he must have been hit in the head with a softball, or kicked by a horse." He brought both hands to his chest as a wide smile spread his lips. "Now me, I'd rather have *you* near my side than a stupid hat left sitting in the cab of my truck."

Shellie fingered the beads on her chest. "Humph! That guy has some nerve. He made it a federal crime that you left with his stupid hat..."

The repeated thoughts of the hat brought along a cache of sensory images, Ben's scent, their first dance, the taste of his kisses, the warmth that flashed in his eyes. Her anger pooled and turned her thoughts to mud. She puffed out a long breath. "Well, it *was* autographed."

The pirate and the starlet stared at her. Patrick sighed and shook his head. He leaned toward Shellie, but Alex wasn't able to hear what he whispered in her friend's ear. A moment later, Shellie nodded.

"What?" Alex asked.

"Nothing," the starlet replied with a picture-perfect, Paparazzi smile.

"Fine, don't tell me." Alex started walking again, picking up her pace.

"See," Patrick said. "She's much prettier mad than when she's feeling sorry for him."

Alex skidded to a halt, hands on her hips and elbows jutted out. "*I* don't have any sympathy for Ben. I was just trying to understand, thinking maybe if the situation was reversed, and it had been me who lost that particular hat—"

"You would have punched him in the stomach and then demanded to know why he had taken it,"

Shellie interrupted.

She tossed her hands high into the air. "For Pete's sake, I was thirteen when I punched Harvey Hammer—and, you have to admit, the kid had it coming."

Patrick tipped his head. "I can't believe a sweet little thing like you would succumb to violence."

"It was an Al Unser, Jr. hat. Besides, I barely tapped his belly, but he howled like a stuck pig."

The three laughed with merriment all around, and Alex succumbed to a lighter mood.

When they reached a fork in the trail, Alex stopped. "Our tent is just up the road." Her gaze locked with Patrick's. "I'm pretty sure we can make it the rest of the way alone. But thank you."

"You're one lovely wench...and you're welcome."

Alex's smile slid into a grin.

"We're not that far apart." Patrick pointed down the road. "Do you see the school bus made into a camper?"

Alex and Shellie nodded.

"We're right down the road from them. Mike has the red pick-up and Ben has a black one...*I've* got the Harley."

Alex's eyebrows shot up. She grabbed his arm, her voice tinged with excitement. "You rode up to the festival on a hog? I was telling Shellie that's what we should do next year—rent bikes and ride up."

The pirate's arms looped around her neck. "I could take you for a ride sometime." He planted a kiss on the top of her forehead. "Will you wait for me? I'd like to hang out some more."

Alex straightened his bandana. "How about I catch up with you later."

He pulled her tight. "Wait for me. It'll only take a minute to tell Laurie and Julia the whereabouts of Mike and Ben." His eyebrow twitched and his finger brushed the tiny white buttons that trailed down the front of her shirt. "Besides, I'm sure it'll take you some time with all those buttons—"

She laughed. *What a flirt.* Alex placed her hand against his chest. No tingle beneath her palm, no quickening of her heart when she looked into his eyes. "Okay, but just friends."

"We'll see." He winked, kissed the tip of her nose and jogged off down the path. "Wait for me."

The Girl Scout giggled and jabbed her in the ribs. "I think you found a replacement for the cowboy."

"Patrick's fun, but he's definitely in the friendship column." The corner of her mouth drooped. Unfortunately, the only name in the other column—ever—was Ben's.

A few minutes later, while changing in the tent, they heard the distinct sound of a puttering golf cart echoing around them.

Shellie lunged through the nylon doorway.

"Be careful," Alex shouted. A second later, the starlet flew back through the opening in the canvas.

"Hurry! Joe's going to take us out to eat and then he'll give us a ride to the concert." She slipped off the necklace, pulled a big hooded sweatshirt over her top and, quicker than Houdini, was out of shorts, into jeans and once again wearing the necklace.

Alex flipped through the clothes in her bag. "You go on without me. I'm going to wait for Patrick. We can all meet up at the inflatable beer can later...say at seven?"

Shellie giggled. "Okay, but stay away from that pirate's plank."

A grin pulled at her lips. "Yeah, well, you keep your hands off Joe's *clubs.*"

"Are you saying I shouldn't drive the wood?" Shellie laughed outright.

Alex responded by tossing the Victoria's Secret bag at her.

"Ooooh, great idea." The starlet quickly made her costume change. "I feel sexier already." She stuck her chest out, but the effect was lost under the oversized sweatshirt.

Alex nodded anyway. "Damn sexy."

Shellie's cheeks were the same color as the beads that bounced on her chest. "See ya." She burst through the tent flap.

Alex slipped into jeans and a fitted white T-shirt and smiled at her friend's good fortune. The Girl Scout with the Boy Scout sure made a cute couple.

She paced around the campfire pit with a diet soda in her hand. After a couple of laps, she gave up and went to find Patrick.

She headed down the trail, and spotted the camper-school bus, pick-up trucks and the Harley. The sight of the hog sent a shiver of excitement through her. She had never ridden, but could imagine the freedom of the wind flowing through her hair and the rumble beneath her legs.

"Patrick?" She walked into the campsite, heard a zipper and turned around. Not Patrick. Just her luck, the name-calling redhead.

The woman stumbled from the tent with Ben's hat on her head and a grin wider than Texas. "You're just in time." She swayed close to the fire. Taking the hat from her head, she fanned the flames. "This time *you* won't be giving the hat back."

"You're crazy." Alex stepped closer. "You're going to burn the hat if—"

The redhead cackled. "That's the plan. Ben's going to be pissed when I tell him you came into camp and stole his hat, and this time you won't be giving it back because..." She stumbled back a step and tossed the hat. "All that will be left is ashes."

The Stetson looked like a deformed Frisbee as it sailed over the campfire and dropped within reach of Alex's feet. She rushed forward and grabbed the brim. "You are seriously nuts."

Julia swayed. "Give me back my hat," she shrieked and stumbled toward Alex.

She gripped the hat tighter. "No way."

The angry redhead's arms churned, her fists plummeted and her shoes kicked up dirt as she started to move.

Alex backed up as the drunken woman's eyes glazed over. Without warning, Julia dropped to the ground, face first.

Alex's mouth hung open. She had never seen anything like that. It wasn't like Julia fainted. She just fell like a sack of potatoes. *Maybe she's dead?* Alex's eyes grew larger as she stared at the motionless form less than a foot from her.

Absentmindedly, she put the hat on her head and cautiously crouched to lean closer. The pungent smell of booze assaulted her nose and her eyes watered. *Dead all right—dead drunk. Figures.*

The redhead groaned and struggled to sit up. Blood spurted from her nose.

Alex reached out. "It might be best if you lie back down."

"Why?" She blinked.

"You have a bloody—"

Julia's hands flew to her face and she screamed. "Help me! Help me!" her voice shrilled, her eyes half-crazed. "Get her away from me. She tried to kill me. Help! *Help!*"

Two men rushed onto the scene and glared at Alex.

"She fell," Alex tried to explain.

The man with a white cowboy hat helped Julia into a sitting position. "Hank, get a towel."

"Sure thing." The other man jogged away.

"It was an accident." Alex stared at the blood and the mess, certain the woman's nose was broken.

"She pushed me!" The redhead had her fists

clenched into balls. "Let me up."

The man turned to Alex. "I think you've done enough, why don't you go." His tone of voice completely changed as he slid his arm around Ben's girl. "Shhh, it'll be fine."

A security guard in a golf cart pulled up. "What's going on?"

Before she could say a word, the man in the white cowboy hat spouted, "Didn't see it, but this woman claims that she"—he pointed an accusing finger at Alex—"threw her to the ground."

"She's a lying, cheating, hat-stealing whore." Blood dripped from Julia's mouth. "And violent, too. She ripped my man's hat from my hands and slammed me down to the ground."

A crowd had gathered, and their accusatory stares raked over Alex. She pulled the hat tighter to her head. *If I give Ben's hat back, the crazy redhead's gonna burn it for sure.* She wasn't about to be blamed a second time.

With the hat secured, her eyebrows drew down and she slowly backed away. There was nothing she could say with the lying bitch's crocodile tears mixing with the blood streaming from her nose. Alex shied away from the onlookers who glared from her to the hat and back again.

She had gotten to the gravel road when the security guard yelled, "You! Wait!"

A flash of ice shot up her spine and her legs shook. She hadn't done anything wrong, yet she wasn't going to stand around until the redheaded hussy convinced them otherwise. Alex's feet started to move before she had completely turned around, and she stumbled, but kept her balance as she jogged away from the campsite.

"Stop!" Another Johnny Flashlight called.

Alex dodged around a group of campers on the gravel road.

"Hey!" Someone yelled. "Stop her!"

She didn't stop or turn around. Instead, she weaved in and out of vacant campsites until her lungs were on fire and her chest heaved. Her heart pounded so loudly she couldn't have heard footsteps if they were right behind her.

Within a clump of trees, she tipped from the waist and gasped for breath. *That woman is nuts.* Her own words echoed back to haunt her, *The next time you or your girlfriend get in my way, I'm going to enjoy knocking you down.* Would everyone think she really had pushed Julia? What if the redhead pressed charges? Alex ground her eyes shut. She had the hat again and Ben already thought she was a thief. There would be no reason for him not to believe Julia. A shiver went up her spine. *Will this nightmare of a weekend never end?*

She slowly slid from the safety of the trees and ventured back to the road. She tried to act casual as she continued to check behind her. Her heart stopped every time something rustled in the shadows. Around every corner and behind every tree she expected to see a security guard.

Where can I go? More than likely, the security guard would alert all the others to watch out for a woman with blue jeans, light brown hair and a white T-shirt heading their way. *He probably told them I was dangerous. With my luck this weekend, I'll probably be tackled by twenty guys wanting to be heroes as soon as I get to the railroad crossing.*

She found a small gravel trail that led through the woods and followed that back to her tent. She only hoped Patrick didn't tell them where she was camped. Her heart slammed in her chest as she climbed inside, hid the Stetson amongst her clothes, quickly changed into a pair of white capris, pulled a pink sweatshirt overtop her T-shirt and slipped on running shoes. She tucked her hair up into a baseball cap. Her hand ran across the small bottle of Jack Daniels, and she slipped that into the waistband of her pants. If she ended up on the run, she was going to need something to keep her warm.

She emerged from the tent and started down the road toward a group of people who were headed in the right direction. She attached herself to the group like a barnacle to a ship, hoping to gain passage to the concert and find Shellie.

She continually reminded herself to *breath and smile* as the rowdy, hooting, hollering mass moved along at a snail's pace.

By the time they got to the railroad crossing, it was impossible to know where one group ended and another began.

She held her breath and kept to the middle of the crowd as they walked by the bored guards at the railroad crossing. Instead of checking to see if anyone was watching her, she kept her eyes focused on the back of man in front of her.

This is crazy. I didn't do anything wrong. It's not like I stole the hat. I'm only protecting my reputation and his property. She pulled the baseball cap tighter on her head. *I wish I'd never come here.* If she could do it all over, she would have burned the stupid hat.

Her last obstacle to overcome would be the security guards at the entrance to the concert. As she waited in line with everyone else, large, lazy raindrops fell. A sudden gust of wind blew past and everything changed. The rain gushed and people rushed, popping up umbrellas and putting on rain gear. A wave of apprehension swept through Alex as she stepped up next to the guard.

He hesitated and took his time looking Alex over. His gaze moved from her knees to her shoulders and back again. She hoped, amongst other things, that he wouldn't find the bottle of Jack Daniels she had secured in the waistband of her pants.

"Ow," Alex yelped as the rain drops hit her. "I feel like I'm being pelted with frozen peas."

The guard chuckled, and with a shake of his hand, he waved her through. The guard nodded his approval and Alex kept her smile to a small grin. She felt like the football player who stepped into the end zone, scoring the winning touchdown, but she knew she had to play it cool. Her pace quickened as the rain fell faster and more umbrellas popped up. She bobbed and weaved her way through the crowd, hoping Shellie would be at the inflatable beer can to meet her. After being jabbed by an elbow and almost speared by an umbrella, she slowed her pace and moved cautiously. To the left stood Ben.

Their eyes locked. She willed her feet to be still as she resisted the urge to race into his arms and explain what had happened to Julia. *It was an accident*, she wanted to shout.

He walked over. "Alex, we need to talk." His eyes were warm as he pushed the brim of her cap back. "I'm so sorry. I was wrong to jump to conclusions. I don't know what I was thinking, and I want you—" The rest of his words were lost in a large clap of thunder.

His tone and touch conveyed heartfelt sincerity and concern. She didn't have to hear the words; she could see the truth in his eyes...and her heart ripped in two. *Why now? Why not so much earlier!* She didn't even care what made him change his mind. Her heart chilled. After Ben heard Julia's lies, she was certain the next time he looked at her, his heart would once again be filled with doubt. *This is so unfair.*

She stood, placed her hands around his neck and slowly drew his lips to hers. When she left the concert, she didn't want to conjure up the hurtful words. She wanted—no, needed—one last, warm kiss to remember.

When their lips met, it wasn't a surge of excitement that rushed through her but a depth of emotion. His mouth and hands seemed to say they were sorry and never wanted to let her go.

The familiar voice of the emcee came through the speakers. "A few announcements for you folks. Will Ben Buck report to the first aid station? Ben Buck, first aid. A black Ford pick up with the plates, 'Her Loss', needs to be moved or it'll be *your* loss..."

He ended the kiss and gave a slight nod toward the gate. "Come on."

"No." She shook her head. "You need to go."

His thumb rested under her chin and his dark eyes held her more firmly then his hands could.

"Come with me."

"I can't," she choked. "She's telling everyone I pushed her down and stole the hat."

"What?" His eyes narrowed.

The split in her heart widened. "I-I have to go." She needed to get away before the memory of their last kiss was tarnished. His arms wrapped around her. Alex braced her hands against his chest and pushed. When his grip loosened, she took a step back. She started to run as his voice bellowed her name. A clap of thunder drowned out any other words, leaving only the remnants of his voice to echo through her mind.

Ben's touch haunted her as she ducked around an umbrella and kept moving.

Alex swallowed, hard. Tears pricked the back of her eyelids. She pushed the thoughts of the kiss away as she concentrated on the task at hand. She needed to find Shellie and get out of here.

Damn! What was she thinking? Her white pants glowed. If she had wanted to blend in, she should have left her jeans on. She needed to hurry and find Shellie. It wouldn't take security long to pick her out of this crowd.

She wound her way through the masses as the announcer's voice boomed through the speakers.

"The National Weather Service has issued a tornado watch. Remember...a tornado watch means conditions are favorable for tornadoes and severe thunderstorms in and close to the watch area. We will be on the lookout for threatening weather conditions and will inform you of any possible warnings. Thank you."

The crowd cheered as a crack of lightning lit up the sky. Everyone *oohed* and *ahhed* as bright bolts sizzled through the air. Alex didn't care about the storm; she had one goal and one goal only—find Shellie and get the heck out of here.

Alex made her way toward the partially erect giant beer can and spotted Shellie holding up half of an oversized yellow rain slicker—Joe held the other half. She stopped abruptly. Joe was part of the security team. Would he bring her in, or help her get away? *Damn!* The two of them would want her to turn herself in and work everything out—even though she'd never win against a crying, bloody beauty queen like Julia.

A bolt of lightning lit up the sky and Shellie became animated, pointing in Alex's direction. Joe reached for his walkie-talkie and that was all she needed to see. She raced for the exit gate that led to the family camp ground, not wanting to be trapped in the concert bowl once the word got out she'd been spotted. When security got a new description of her clothes, the chances of her slipping by the guards would be slim.

Why is this happening? Everyone is turning against me.

Her eyes stung. Cold, damp air filled her lungs as she stealthily made her way through the crowd. She wasn't going to jail, she was going home. Her legs shook more from fear than cold as she reached up to massage the knotted muscles in her neck. *I'm getting out of here.* She jogged toward the exit on the opposite side of the concert bowl, then slowed down to walk with a family of four carrying chairs and wearing plastic bags with holes cut out for their head and arms. The guards didn't even glance at them as they went out the exit. *Maybe Joe hadn't been reporting me.*

Indecision faltered her steps. *Maybe I should go back and find Shellie?* She kept walking. The thought of taking a chance on Joe was dismissed as soon as she considered the consequences of being wrong. A night in jail with a bunch of drunks was not an option. She tried to get her bearings as she walked down the road leading to the unfamiliar family campgrounds. The chain link fence in the woods behind their campsite butted up to the family campgrounds. It would be a long way around, but if she could get back to her site, she could wait by the fence until morning, then grab her car, and get away during the confusion of everyone leaving. Or, if she could find Shellie, they could pull out tonight under the cover of the storm and dark skies.

Why did Shellie have to fall for a security guard?

Alex saw the headlights before she heard the rumble of the golf cart. She moved back into the shadows, glad the family campsites were quiet. A quarter of the tents she spotted glowed softly, illuminating the families tucked safely inside. Most of the other sites were unoccupied.

Her sweatshirt soaked up water like a sponge, her feet slid on the rain-soaked gravel road and her eyes strained to see her way in dark. If it wasn't for the lightning, she would never have been able to see the small path that headed up into the woods. Alex shivered with indecision. It was a long way up that hill and the woods were dark.

Startled by a noise, she held her breath and turned, half expecting to see the glowing eyes of a wolf, bear or coyote, but there was nothing.

Stop it! You're being paranoid. You can do this. She started up the dark hill with a slow, sure gait, gaining confidence with each step. *You can do this...you can do this.*

A noise echoed through her mantra. She stopped, held her breath and turned, half-expecting to see the eyes of a predator. *Nothing.*

Before her lungs re-filled, a heavy arm slid around her waist. Knees turned to slush and a scream fought its way to her throat. Alex opened her mouth just as warm fingers slid across her lips, stifling her cry for help.

Chapter Fourteen

Alex lashed out with her arms and legs, but she was unable to break the attacker's tight hold. Fear pushed her back and animal instinct had her lunge forward. The hold weakened, she lost her footing, and they both fought to catch their balance before hitting the ground.

The extra weight on her back forced the air from her lungs. The attacker rolled off her as she gasped for breath.

"Alex! It's me, Patrick." He moaned. "What's wrong with you? What are you doing?"

She struggled to sit up; the cool air filled her lungs. "Me?" she puffed, gathering more breath. "What's wrong with *you?*"

She heard the heave of his own breathing as he sat up next to her. Damp fingers brushed the clinging hair from her eyes. "You're the one running around in the dark and rain. Your friend asked me to find you."

Panic well up in her. "I don't want to go to jail."

His fingers gripped her shoulders. "What are you talking about?"

"B-Ben's girlfriend is telling everyone I pushed her down, that I'm a thief, and—"

"Shh, it's going to be okay." His voice was soft and low.

Lightning cracked, thunder boomed and a high-powered flashlight suddenly illuminated them. She shielded her eyes from the glare of the flashlight.

A voice boom in the darkness, "I located her in

the family campground."

She pushed against Patrick. "You tricked me! You helped them find me...let me go!"

They wrestled around, but he held her firm. "Alex, listen to me. I didn't know, I swear." His voice was low. "There's only one guard. We'll run up the hill into the dark, you go to your left and I'll go the right. He can't follow both of us."

Can I trust him? She could only think of two choices, making a run for it or turning herself in. The thought of walking down the hill with her arms extended and being knocked to the ground, handcuffed and hauled off to jail sounded a whole lot less appealing than running. She nodded.

"Okay, on the count of three." He hauled her up by one arm. "One, two, three!"

They took off running, splitting up half way to the top of the hill. Patrick darted to his right, she went left.

Alex stayed off of the roads, using the lightning to show her hidden breaks in between campsites as she made her way up the remainder of the hill. When she came to the chain link fence, she suddenly realized the flaw in Patrick's plan. Trees, campers and tents were butted up to the fence. It would take her three times as long getting around all the obstacles. She had no choice; she'd have to brave the road.

Thunder and lightning continued to put on a show, the sound from the speakers was muffled and she wasn't even sure if the concert was still going on. Sirens blared in the distance. Her pants and sweatshirt soaked with rain and caked with mud, she trembled as the wind blew harder, pelting her with rain, leaves and twigs. Her body shook, but she wasn't sure if it was from fear or the cold. She wanted desperately just to go home.

Her feet slid through the mud as she stepped

back onto the road. She wondered about the sanity of her plan. The curved road went downhill and would take her back to the entrance of the campground. She needed to find a different road and quickly stepped back into the woods where the brush was denser.

Twigs and sticks caught at her face and hair. The thunder roared, the lightning flashed and a tree cracked. The ground shook beneath her. A large whoosh of air pounded her back and propelled her forward. Her footing faltered and she stumbled to her knees. Though her body ached, she knew she couldn't stay here and slowly got to her feet. Alex glanced over her shoulder and stifled a gasp. Not more than twenty yards behind her, a tree had split. *I could have been under that tree.* She shivered.

Alex swallowed hard then hurried back to the road. She no longer cared about getting caught; the fear of being dead in the woods for weeks, decomposing while everyone searched for her, was more frightening than the prospect of landing in the clinker.

Wet leaves slapped her face and stung her cheeks. A flash of lightning had her cringing and fearing the next falling tree. She burst through the trees and brush, holding her hands out in front as she pushed her way to the road. A branch clawed at her sweatshirt. Her heart rose in her chest as something else clamped onto her arm. She screamed.

"Stop it," the voice commanded.

She clamped her mouth shut, muffling the last sounds of fright as nature continued the laser light show. The guard stood a head taller than her.

"Alexandra Coe?"

"Yes." She scrunched her eyes, realizing too late that she had given her identity away. She stepped back.

His fingers dug into her arms. "I've been

instructed to pick you up and bring you back to the trailer."

"Listen," she stammered. "It's not what you think."

"You are Alexandra Coe?"

"Yes, but—" Unsuccessfully, she tried to slip her arm from his grip.

"I've got handcuffs, mace and a stun gun. Don't make me use them."

Eyes widening, her blood turned ice-cold.

"You're coming with me."

He pulled her down the path and she wondered if they did any psychological testing on security guards. This guy didn't seem real stable. She spoke slowly and distinctly. "If you could bring me to Shellie and Joe—he's a security guard. They'll explain this misunderstanding. They're over at the concert bowl." She hoped her voice sounded more confident than she felt.

The guard's grip became bruising. He mumbled something unintelligible as he dragged her to the cart. "Sit," he commanded and released his hold. "Don't try anything stupid. I'm bringing you in."

She leaned back. *What's the use? No matter what I do, it turns out wrong.* Her body shivered beneath the rain-soaked sweatshirt, and with shaking fingers she massaged her aching right arm. *It just doesn't matter anymore.* She didn't even care what direction they went as the golf cart sped down the road, bouncing through the puddles and mud.

After ten minutes, they came to a little cement-block building. With a door and windows made from chain link fencing, the place looked more like a giant dog kennel than a holding pen for criminals. The rain pinged loudly against the aluminum roof as the security guard yanked her from the cart, unlocked the gate and pushed her in.

Alex stumbled inside. The rain splashed through

the chain link and she slunk backward, while her eyes remained fixed on the guard. She stopped when the back of her legs butted up against something. She turned cautiously to find a small cot, blankets and a pillow. The area was dry and out of the reach of the rain and the guard. A ragged breath filled her lungs.

The lock clicked loudly; the sound echoed through her and a shiver of fear spiraled down her spine. Heart pounding harder, her gaze darted to the corners of the cage. She held her breath, certain she'd find the glowing eyes of a wild animal.

His radio blared like an alarm clock. He pressed a button shouting, "Hey, what do I do? Come in...come in?" He waved the device around, banged it against his leg then shouted, "Stupid radio. What am I suppose to do?" The guard brought it back to his mouth. "Hey! Can anyone hear me?" The radio cracked, but no one responded. He stormed to the gate and shook it. "Hey, you. I'll be back so don't try anything stupid."

"Wait!" She rushed forward, more afraid of being abandoned in the woods than of riding in the cart with Rambo. Alex gave the fence a good shake, but the lock didn't tumble off and the door didn't swing open. "You can't leave me alone out in the middle of nowhere, trapped in a cage."

"I told you, I'll be back," he shouted over another clap of thunder, spun around and raced back to the cart.

"Get back here! Unlock the door, now!" He didn't even glance back as he took off in the cart.

Another dose of anger and fear was added to her raging emotions. She slid slowly back as her shoulders shrunk. *He abandoned me.* She yanked the heavy, wet sweatshirt over her head and then pulled one of the blankets off the bed. Her limbs trembled with emotion and fatigue as she held it tightly around her shoulders.

Headlights of a cart flashed through the wire fencing of the window. Lightning illuminated two people in the front seat. *Joe? Shellie?* She prayed her friends were coming to bust her loose. As the cart got closer, she could make out a big, burly man driving. Her stomach pitted then heaved as he stopped the cart in front of the door. With quick, efficient moves, he yanked the person in a black rain slicker out of the passenger seat, unlocked the gate and tossed him inside before Alex could even blink. The guy stumbled and fell forward onto his knees as the guard relocked the gate.

"Hey, where are you going?" she yelled. "Stop, you can't leave us here!"

She didn't know if the guard didn't hear over the booming thunder, or didn't care. She backed to the corner as the person in black struggle to stand.

"I could use a little help, here. They've got my hands tied together." The deep male voice under the black plastic was eerily familiar. He gave his body a shake and sent water spraying from the rain slicker.

Alex stood motionless with her back plastered against the cement-block wall.

He gave his head another shake. "What's the matter, can't you hear?" The hood slid off and their eyes locked. "*You!*" His expression clouded in anger. "I suppose I should just lie down so you can kick the crap out of me. I hear you're pretty good at beating up drunks."

Her lips thinned and her nostrils flared. "I *did not* beat up your girlfriend."

"Innocent people don't run away." His cold voice boomed as loud as the thunder. "And my hat is missing...again."

"Technically, it's my hat. You gave it to me last year." She stepped over to where he knelt and narrowed her eyes as she sunk to his level. "I didn't rip the hat from your head, mister. *You* placed it on mine, remember?" She watched his nostrils flare and heard the quick intake of his breath.

And then, just as quick, his eyes went from cold stone black to warm brown and inviting.

"Yeah, I do. But you're always running from me." His voice as soft as a whisper. "Every time I think..." His facial features hardened. "Never mind."

"No, no, you're wrong." Frustration caused her body to tremble while the cold set her teeth chattering. "I-I came here looking for you...but you wouldn't listen."

"To lies."

"No, no. That's just it. I've been telling the truth—unlike your girlfriend. If you would have...only—"

He shook his head. "How can I believe you when...?"

Her spine stiffened, and this time, she held her ground. "If I told you Julia was going to burn the hat and I only took the Stetson to keep it safe, would you believe me?"

"Would you believe me if I told you the hat was for my brother. He has Down's syndrome, and Toby Keith is his favorite artist."

They had spoken at the same time. The sudden silence seemed louder than the rain as they remained on their knees, nose-to-nose and unblinking, searching for answers, for the truth.

The muscles in Alex's legs twitched as cold soaked deeper into her bones, but she wouldn't give in, wouldn't move away, or stand up. *Why can't he say he believes I'm telling the truth?* Her heart hammered and her resolve slipped. *Does he really have a brother? Was that the only reason he did the charity bull ride...even with me as a partner?* His breath was hot against her lips and cheek, sending a different kind of chill down her spine.

She nodded. "I do—" Her words were drowned out by a deafening roar and a ground-shaking crash. Her thoughts scattered and her eyes grew larger. Rain drops pelted them and the wind roared.

"Go!" Ben shouted, frantically pointing with clasped hands to the corner.

Alex didn't think twice, she yanked him to his feet. The plastic rain poncho ripped and fell to the ground. Her fingers dug into his flesh as her feet tried to gain traction in her attempt to race backward, pulling him with her. They tumbled into the corner just as a tree pierced the chain link. Plastered against the back wall, his body covered hers like a shield as hail the size of baseballs pounded the floor and leaves, twigs and rain pelted them. Was her life meant to end here at Country Time, in a building with the one person she thought she had wanted to spend the rest of her life with?

As quickly as the howling winds started, they stopped. Branches, leaves and jagged ice chunks littered the cement floor. The rain still pounded against the roof, but the intensity diminished.

"Are you okay?" His voice was warm against her neck, his words soft.

She nodded, her throat tight with emotion, his presence, and another narrow escape.

Ben shuffled to stand. "Are you sure?"

She nodded, stood and pulled the blanket tighter. Her thoughts and emotions were scattered like the leaves and twigs from the storm. She shifted her weight gently from foot to foot. *It'll take years to sort through the feelings and memories left from this weekend.* Her body ached with the need to be wrapped in his arms and comforted.

He kicked at a chunk of hail as the silence between them grew awkward.

Finally, Ben cleared his throat. "I bet the winds had to be going at least eighty miles an hour when they ripped through here."

"Oh my God!" Images of the starlet spinning like Dorothy from the Wizard of Oz had her voice rising in fear. "If Shellie went back to the tent to look for me and a..." She shivered.

"Hey, hey." His tethered hands reached out for her. His voice filled with warmth and concern. "Your friend's safe. They were keeping everyone in the concert bowl."

"If anything happened to her, I don't know what I'd do."

"She'll be fine." His voice was warm as his thumb brushed her upper arm.

Unnerved by the concern reflected in his eyes she struggled for something to say. *What if he hadn't heard her earlier?* Should she repeat that she believed him when he said he had a brother and the hat was for him?

After everything she'd been through this weekend, her heart couldn't take much more. If he thought she was a liar, she'd rather have his contempt than his concern. With his scorn, she could slam the door on that chapter of her life, but his tenderness would create a void filled with what ifs. Too fragile to confess again and run the risk of him slamming her heart to the ground and stomping on it by calling her a liar, her mind fumbled for a safer subject. "Why are your wrists zip-corded together?" she stammered.

Ben held his hands up and let out a chuckle. "The Johnny Flashlight that hauled me in was a little too eager to make an arrest."

"At least you didn't get Rambo." She smirked. "I'm surprised my hands and feet aren't shackled."

"What did he do to you?" His voice grew low and stern as he turned toward the gate.

Her heart grasped for hope at his protective stance and she brushed a hand over his forearm until he stopped and turned back around.

With a slight shake of her head she said, "Nothing, just a lot of threats. The handcuffs, you know—"

Their gazes met, locked. After a few minutes, a small smile appeared and a touch of humor shown from his eyes. "It's my own fault. I was pissed off and taunted the guy. Held my hands out and dared him." His laughter rumbled along with the receding thunder. "Thank God I didn't suggest that he pat me down."

Alex breathed easier as his smile deepened.

That look on his face caused heat to radiate throughout her body. She only wished *he* wanted to crush her to his chest with a need so strong that he'd be powerless to resist the physical pull between the two of them. She wanted him to tremble as she did, trying to curb his desire...for her. *Why couldn't he want me the way I need him?*

Ben's eyes shot wide. "Of course, being a rent-a-cop, he never thought to check me for weapons." His voice turned serious as he held her gaze. "I'm going to show how much I trust you. There's a pocket-knife in my front pocket. Just reach in and pull it out."

Alex stepped away, her pulse quickening. The thought of standing chest to chest and working her fingers into his pocket had her face flushed. This wouldn't be a lingering moment, this would be one more memory etched forever into her heart.

Her lungs quickly filled with air and she shook her head. *No way.* Weak as her emotions were, her hand would slide into his pocket, she'd wrap her free arm around his waist and make a complete fool of herself.

"Come on, I think I'm losing feeling in my hands. How would you feel if they had to amputate my hands because you wouldn't help?" he cajoled. His brown eyes softened along with his words.

With false bravado, she spoke loudly. "Someone should be back for us any minute. Besides, they wouldn't use the plastic strips for handcuffs if people got injured." She glanced at his hands just to confirm they weren't rotting off his wrists.

"Those guys are just rent-a-cops. They don't know the first thing about putting these on. *Besides*, no one is coming out here to get us—by the time the Police find time after this storm, it'll be next Thursday."

"The security guards will come back. They have to." Even to her own ears, her voice sounded more hopeful than confident. She bit her lower lip and surveyed the debris rather than look him in the eyes. She didn't want to stay in this giant dog kennel for a week. She needed to check on Shellie and she'd need to undo his hands for him to help.

He moved slowly. "They're not coming back." He spoke in an odd yet gentle tone. He slid forward, stopping a foot from her. "There will be trees across the roads, crowd control and the cell phone lines will be jammed with everyone trying to make calls back home." He held his hands out to her. "Please."

She studied the strip of white plastic that dug into his skin. Her fingers reached out to touch the cord. It was stiff and hard. She brushed his skin. It was tight. Her stomach was heavy with thoughts of Ben being in pain. Her gaze traveled to his eyes, the corners crinkled in amusement. Apparently his suffering wasn't too great. She had half a mind to leave his hands tied. "First, you have to tell me why you were so pissed that you taunted the guard."

The toe of his boot pushed a twig around and he shrugged. "I went to push Patrick, but he kind of lowered his head, and instead of my hand connecting with his chest...I punched him in the face." He straightened and tilted his hip toward her. "Now will you get the knife?"

She held up her hand. "I thought you were friends. Why were you pushing him—punching him?"

His smile slipped. "Close calls make you start to think."

Her heart pounded. *Believe me, I know.* Close calls make the truth that much more important. "Are you really a cowboy?"

Ben leaned closer, the corner of his mouth tipped. "We're locked in a cell, and you want to know if I'm a cowboy. I could see asking if I was a lock smith..."

"Guess that was a stupid question?" Her gaze dipped to the ground. "What I really want to know..." Her cheeks burned and she hoped he couldn't see. "About Julia..." She paused again not sure how to ask.

"Hey, don't worry about her. She's fine. And, for the record, I don't believe you ran into camp, went into my truck, stole the hat and then slammed her to the ground."

"What do you see in her?" She cringed. "I didn't just say that aloud, did I?"

He laughed. "Yep, I heard that. Actually, I only invited her up as a favor to my buddy Mike. But don't worry. By next weekend, they'll once again have me paired up with another woman who's supposed to be perfect."

Her limbs were as heavy as the sweatshirt she discarded to the floor. She didn't want to hear any more and quickly changed the subject. "Your brother—"

A soft smile touched his lips. "His name is Dustin, and he loves Toby Keith," he said proudly.

The blanket slipped from her shoulders. "I didn't know. And I didn't mean to take the hat last year, honest." A wave of sadness swept through her. She blinked and swallowed back the pain. *Had she just been a weekend thing to him?* "I was trying to return the hat."

His thumb slid gently across her cheek before brushing her bottom lip. "I shouldn't have said that. I'm sorry." His voice was low and filled with regret. His hand rested on her shoulder. "But I'm glad *you* came back."

Not that the hat came back, but...her. Alex shuddered as hope slipped back into her heart.

Time ticked by. They were so close. Her tongue moistened her lips as she waited for his kiss.

The corners of her mouth tipped up as he lifted his arms higher. His shirt rode up to expose a trim waist and snug jeans. "Now, about my hands?"

Her heart sunk. He wasn't going to kiss her.

With a devilish glint in his eye, he stepped closer.

There wasn't a lot of room to maneuver, between the bed and cinder-block walls. She sidestepped the water-soaked branch that pierced the chain link fence and jutted across the floor.

"A deal's a deal." His voice was steady, his eyes forceful and his grin disarming. "Cut me loose."

She shook her head and stepped back. He moved closer.

The back of her legs bumped against the bed frame; she was trapped. His knees knocked against her legs, and before she could react, his bound arms went up and over her head like a hula-hoop, pinning her arms to his side. The blanket slid to the floor and her breasts rubbed against his chest.

She immediately started to struggle.

"Ow! Stop," he yelled. "You'll rip my arms from their sockets."

The sensation of his muscles rippling against her chest had her confused as to whose heart was pounding. "Serves you right," she said breathlessly.

"Will you help me?" His gaze was as soft as a

caress.

Her heart jolted. Her pulse pounded. "I can't help you, my arms are stuck." Her lips accidentally brushed against his neck as she spoke. The sensation of his pulse pounding beneath her lips had her going back to the same spot. Although this time, it wasn't an accident, more an act of involuntary necessity. Excitement rippled through her. *He did say he was sorry.* The weekend that had been so wrong, suddenly seemed so right. She leaned into him, wanting to be closer and needing his arms to hold her.

Her lips sought out the spot. Her heart danced with excitement as his bound arms nestled in the small of her back. His fingers brushed against her bottom. He drew her closer and a hot ache clung in her throat.

His fingers slid over her barred skin, and desire surged as her mind shouted warnings. *Be careful, you don't know what is real anymore.* As she slid slowly under his arms, her breasts rubbed against his chest. She kissed the hard planes and sunk closer to the floor. She wasn't sure, but she thought she moaned. He stood as still as a statute as she boldly made her way out of his arms. Her palm warmed as heat permeated through his jeans. She rose and swallowed. Her skin tingled and her mouth ached with a need to touch and taste, to run her lips from his strong chin down across his chest. Her hands wanted to caress his skin, not run along the outside of his clothing. She wanted to feel his arms hold her tight as he pressed his body to hers.

But first, she needed to free his hands.

She moved her fingers over his thigh. His muscle was hard and firm beneath her touch. As she moved toward his waist, her hand ran over something hard and she froze. *Was that the knife?*

His warm lips brushed her cheek. "Mmm-hmmm."

Her skin tingled, need pulsated through her veins.

Light kisses against her skin, motivated her to free his hands. She forced her fingers into his pocket.

"Oh," he groaned.

He turned his head; his tongue traced the outline of her ear and a shiver shot down to her toes. Her left arm went around his waist as her fingers clutched his firm butt. Slowly, she stuffed her fingers further into his front pocket. "Oh, God," she moaned as she rubbed across what *wasn't* his knife.

The pounding pulse in her head drowned out the words he murmured. Her right hand searched for the knife. Her breath became labored as she tried to remember that she was only looking for a pocket knife.

A low sound, a mixture of both pleasure and agony, escaped from his throat as her fingers wrapped around the pocket knife. She worked hard to free the object from the constraints of his damp denim pocket. All she wanted was to cut him loose and plaster her body to his.

The knife trembled in her hand. His thigh brushed against her hip and he pressed closer. She curbed her desire long enough to pull out the shiny blade. She placed it under the hard white plastic band and applied pressure, but the cord didn't give. "I wish I had my wire cutters or—"

"What would a pretty girl like you be doing with wir—"

"Hey, men might not find me attractive, but they drool over my collection of tools at the garage..."

"You're wrong." His voice had softened.

The knife stilled. "No, I'm not. I've got everything from a—"

"No, not about the tools." He laughed. "Men must drool over you. You're beautiful."

"You're just saying that because I have the knife," she bantered, uncomfortable with the compliment.

"Only one way to prove me wrong. Cut me loose and hand back the knife."

With the knife edge up against the plastic, she sawed, nodded and played along. "I'll quickly cut you loose, hand back the knife and wait for all the words to describe my beauty."

The moment the tie hit the ground, his hands wrapped around her waist, pulling her tight against him. "Your eyes are sexy." His thumb brushed her cheek. "Soft skin and warm." He traced the outline of her ear and pushed a pigtail from her shoulder, "Great hair and cute ears."

The knife slipped from her fingers and fell with a ping against the cement floor.

He didn't appear to notice as his fingers massaged her shoulders. "Strong, fit." His lips grazed her neck. "And, oh, so delectable." His hands slowly slid down the length of her sides and lingering right above the swell of her bottom.

Her chest brushed up against him. She pressed her lips together and stifled the moans and groans. Every nerve ending vibrated with the need to feel his lips on hers.

His hand slipped beneath her waistband and snagged on the forgotten bottle of Jack Daniels.

"What's this?" His eyebrows arched as he held the brown plastic flask to view.

A smile flirted across her lips. "It looks like a bottle." She snatched it, slipped it into her back pocket and moved closer, trembling from excitement, nerves and need.

"You're cold?" His reached down and picked up the blanket that had slid to the ground. "You need to get out of those wet clothes." His eyebrows arched high and the corners of his mouth slid up into a sexy, wild grin that sucked the breath from her lungs.

Her skin went from cold to hot everywhere he touched. If his hands didn't stop, steam would soon billow off her. She murmured and gave a slight shake of her head.

Ignoring her weak protest, he quickly wrapped the blanket around her. "Want me to take off your pants?" The corner of his mouth twitched deliciously.

"I want you to kiss me." She opened the blanket and drew him inside, claiming his lips.

Ben crushed her against him. While his tongue sent shivers of desire racing through her, his hand cupped her butt before rising to slip the bottle from her pocket. His lips left hers to nibble at her earlobe and he murmured, "*Whiskey girl. My little whiskey girl.*"

His voice sent shivers down her spine.

"I've got just the trick to warm you up." He took a sip from the bottle, then his lips were on hers. The sensation was fire and ice. She held fast to his mouth and the whiskey. Another sip and a kiss, and her knees went weak.

"Your turn." He held the bottle up.

She took a swig, and with a mouth full of Jack, kissed him. The liquor splashed and she was off on a scavenger hunt tracking down the errant drops. Her tongue followed the liquor trail racing across his chin and down his neck. His arms encircled her waist and his fingers painted images across her back. Before she could splash a little more whiskey on his neck, he dipped her backwards. The bottle flew from her hand, and sprinkled them in liquor.

"My turn." His eyes blazed with passion and he kissed her everywhere. Blood leapt from her heart, pounded in her head and made her knees tremble. Her body pressed closer, and she melted into his strength. She not only wanted Ben, she needed him. He was the half to her whole. She wanted to whisper into his ear how much she had missed him and wanted him. But pride kept her from verbalizing her thoughts. She didn't want to scare him off with declarations of passion.

His arm slipped beneath her knees. Before she could murmur a protest, her feet came off the ground and he cradled her in his arms like she weighed no more than a sack of potatoes. She wrapped her arms around his neck and he spun her around.

She laughed and begged. "Stop, set me down."

Another quick turn and he gently lowered her to the bed. "Your wish is my command." He slid down beside her on the narrow cot.

Her heart sung out, *yes*. She reveled in his hard planes pressed up against her curves. The winds picked up and pelted the roof with fat raindrops. Thunder boomed and lightning flashed.

They snuggled closer. Ben tucked the blanket around her shoulder. "Better?"

She nodded and tried to read the look in his eyes. His touch turned tentative. His lips hovered just beyond her reach. What was he thinking? Was he taking advantage of the moment while he wondered about who he'd be with next weekend?

His finger trailed across the wrinkles in her forehead. "You're thinking way too hard. Don't worry. We'll get out of here."

She closed her eyes, not wanting him to see that she'd fallen for him all over again.

His lips brushed her cheek. "It'll be okay, I promise."

She let her mind go blank and drank in the sensation of his kiss and the tingle that vibrated with his touch. His lips trailed across her cheeks, he nuzzled her jaw line and lingered on her ear lobe. The blanket slipped from her shoulder. She scooted closer, amazed at how their bodies fit beautifully together. They were truly made for each other. The heat from his hand penetrated through her wet pants and she squirmed.

He nuzzled her neck. His lips hit her collar bone and she sucked in air. His hot tongue didn't stop there. It continued a slow assault, moving from her shoulder to the inside of her elbow and searing down to her palm. Her toes curled and the bed squeaked.

She opened her eyes and watched his finger gingerly touch her tattoo. He edged up on his elbow, his brows drawn together in concentration.

Her palms brushed his ears and she pulled his face close. *Don't go there,* she silently pleaded. The confusion in his eyes turned to tenderness.

She slipped her hand under his shirt and kissed his neck. He shifted and she found herself cradled in his arms.

"You didn't have that tattoo last year."

Alex paused and held her breath, not wanting this conversation, not now, not here.

"Your mom is the Coe woman that was hit by the train last year in Kakato Township the last night of Country Time," he continued, his voice lowering to almost a caressed whisper. "That's why you left, isn't it?"

She stiffened and struggled out of his arms. He grabbed the blanket and tried to wrap it around her.

Alex pushed his hands away, pulled her knees tight to her chest and pulled the blanket shut. "Don't say it." She rocked. A hot tear rolled down her cheek and she closed her eyes, trying to swallow the pain.

Ben's thumb touched her cheek. "I'm sorry. "

She slapped at his hand. She didn't want his pity.

"I didn't know," he whispered.

She kept her eyes closed and her head down. *It's not fair*. Pride straightened her back. Why didn't he say he wanted her, or that he missed her and she was in his thoughts for the last year. She attempted

193

to swallow the hurt.

"Alex," he said tenderly. "I don't know what to say. I feel bad."

"Do me a favor..." her voice quivered.

"Anything."

"Leave me alone." She spoke the words with finality.

He leaned back. "Why? I don't understand."

Ignoring him, she gently rocked, shielding her face from his view. She didn't want him seeing her hurt and in pain. She'd rather be in jail amongst strangers than stuck in this room with him.

Life wasn't fair. She'd wanted his passion...not his pity.

Chapter Fifteen

"I'm so sorry." Ben reached out to hold her, but she cringed back, pain evident in her wary eyes. *Why won't she let me comfort her?*

Alex's body went rigid and she pulled away even further. "Don't you understand? I don't want your pity."

He stood slowly, reached into his pocket and held out a stick of gum. "Want a piece?"

"No," she whispered.

He popped the piece into his mouth and almost choked on the sour taste that caught in his mouth. He tried to swallow. How could she think pity motivated his actions? His toe pushed around a piece of hail while he searched for answers. The mess from the storm mirrored his insides. The pit of his stomach burned with the knowledge that he had contributed to her pain.

His fingers trailed through his hair. All he wanted was to hold her in his arms, comfort her, and show her how much she meant to him. "If I could, I'd turn back the hands on the clock for you."

She glanced up. "How far back?"

"To the moment your eyes sparkled green and a sweet smile spread across your lips." His fingers trailed under her chin and he offered a grin. "Come on, let me see a little smile," he cooed as if she were a child.

The tips of her fingers were white from clutching the blanket, and her lowered lashes obscured those beautiful eyes. "You can't change the past."

His hands massaged her shoulders. "Alex," he spoke softly. When she didn't respond, he changed his approach. "Can't we at least be friends?" he teased.

She looked him in the eye and he knew immediately he had said the wrong thing.

"Shit."

Her skin vibrated beneath his hand, her bottom lip trembled and her teeth chattered. He figured it was more than the cold that caused her to shiver.

He pulled the shirt off his body and slid her head through the opening. "It's dry and should help a little."

She sat staring blankly. He wasn't even sure if she knew he was there. She was a million miles away as she sat motionless. He pried the blanket from her fingers and pushed her arms through the openings like he'd done a million times for Dustin. The only difference was his brother would thank him, whereas Alex grasped for the blanket, cocooning herself inside.

He tried to swallow, but couldn't. Her knees were pulled tight to her chest. Did she hate him? Could he blame her?

His stomach tightened as the roof groaned loudly above them. "We should leave and get you some place safe and warm." His insides somersaulted. Why couldn't that place be in his arms?

Reluctantly, he left her, side-stepped the branch that pierced the fence and examined the lock on the gate. He might not know what to say, but he knew he could get them out of there. When he lifted the water-soaked branch, the green leaves sent up a spray of water as he used the thick stock to spring the gate from the hinges. "Come on," he shouted. "We're breaking out of this joint."

Not even a grin. *So much for trying to make her smile.*

He swiped the wet leaves from his hair and brushed the droplets from his face as he walked back and helped her stand. Her eyes were dry and unblinking. He would have preferred tears to her withdrawn silence.

The blanket slid from her shoulders and he readjusted the rough material, tucking the corner around her like a beach towel. Her body stiffened as he used his arm to propel her forward.

As Ben led her down the muddy road, the sound of blaring sirens increased and the noise of a chopper filled the air. A spotlight shined through the woods, and he wondered what they were looking for.

"The lightning must have knocked the power out." He pointed in the direction of the darkened concert bowl.

Alex stopped, her complexion ghost white in the storm-ravaged moonlight. "Shellie."

"It's okay." With steady pressure on her back, he got her started back down the path. "We're going to find your friend. She'll be all right."

"You don't know that." Her words were flat.

"And you don't know that she won't be," he countered.

The silence between them hung like a dense fog, the words he needed to say obscured from his vision.

As he got them through the unmanned checkpoint, his stomach clenched tight. Time was running out for him. He wanted to wrap her in his arms and kiss her, but the thought of her pushing him away again kept him still next to her. If their last moment together wasn't going to be filled with promise and passion, at least he'd be sure she was safe.

The whirl of generators, emergency lights and first aid stations melded with the crowd of ragged and silent concert goers. He had no idea how anyone would find someone.

Alex, on the other hand, must have had a plan because he no longer needed to push her forward. Ben picked up his pace as his arm slid slightly from her shoulder. It might be the last time he'd touch her and he wanted to prolong this moment of pleasure and pain. His jaw slacked as he searched the crowd of people. He didn't see anyone who was injured, but their open-mouth, wide-eyed stares were just as concerning.

As Ben followed Alex's lead, he searched the subdued crowd. He hoped his friends had stayed in the concert bowl after he'd been taken by the security guard. His steps faltered as he cranked his body halfway around. *Was that Mike?* He stopped and squinted to his right. *Nope.* Realizing his arm embraced only air, he picked up his pace and caught up with Alex. His arm slid back around her shoulders. She didn't even acknowledge his touch; instead, she moved faster. He matched her steps, not wanting to lose her.

His jaw dropped. Stunned, he watched her fly into Patrick's arms. Ragged pain seared his chest.

Patrick glanced up, one eye black and swollen. "What the hell happened to you two?" His brows narrowed as his arms wrapped protectively around a shuddering Alex. "Shhhhh, it's okay."

"I got tossed into a make-shift holding cell with Alex. After the guards left, I was able to bust us out." His right hand brushed Alex's shoulder. "Do you want me to look for your friend?"

The hope of her nod faded when she didn't move from Patrick's embrace.

"Don't bother. Shellie's helping out at the first aid station near the women's bathrooms. She asked me to wait here for Alex."

"Have you seen or heard from Mike, Laurie—"

"Yeah, everyone's fine. Mike offered his assistance to some of the security guards who are working to clear the roads. Laurie and Julia are holed up in Rick's RV."

"That's good at least."

Patrick patted Alex's back as if she were a small child. "Are you two all right?"

"Yeah, we're fine." There was no way he could stand around and watch Patrick comfort her. He reached out and brushed the back of her head, needing the connection one more time. "Guess I should go help Mike with clearing the road."

Her head turned and their eyes met. She shifted and hope welled inside.

"Thank you." Her voice was no more than a whisper.

"You don't need to thank me." He smiled, and brushed her cheek with his thumb. "Alex, I swear I'll make this up to you."

Her smile was sweet, her eyes wary yet softening.

This isn't goodbye, he silently promised them both. With a final nod, he walked toward the exit.

He had let his ego and pride overrule his heart this whole weekend—the entire past year. Instead of jumping to conclusions, he should have taken a moment to consider other possibilities. Why had he been so eager to believe the worst? Why couldn't he have trusted his own feelings...the ones he had the first time he held her in his arms.

Stupid, stupid boy.

****

Chainsaws buzzed and voices grew louder but Alex didn't care, she just wanted to go home.

"The road clearing crews must be near our campsite," Shellie shouted over the noise.

The area ahead was illuminated with spotlights, flashlights and the headlights from golf carts while

199

all around them the roadway was littered with debris. Alex folded her arms tight across her chest. The material from Ben's shirt rubbed across her bare skin and his touch came back.

Her body reacted before her mind formed a thought, and her throat tightened with emotion. If a silly shirt could turn her on, how would she ever get him out of her head? She was so confused. High school had been easier. The boys in high school liked her because she could fix a car. And Ben liked her because—what? Because her mom was dead? His hugs and kisses had been nothing more than a reaction to the situation; she could have easily been a cute puppy he stooped to pat on the head. *Poor puppy. Poor Alex.* She bit her lip against the painful memories.

The noise stopped, and a voice boomed with an eerie echo. "All right, after we clear away the next thirty feet of road, we'll be at the top of the hill. That's where we'll call it a night and reconvene at first light. Those of you who don't have shelter can find a place to rest at the concert bowl."

"Poor beauty," one worker suddenly muttered.

"What a shame," another whispered as more nameless condolences littered the air. A saw engine revved up and the chorus of noise started again.

A chill raced up Alex's spine, and she rushed past Shellie. Their campsite was blocked by the muscled backs of a dozen or so men.

The hairs on the back of her neck tingled. With an urgent need, she pushed through the crowd, stopping with a horrified stillness when her car came into view.

The overhead light shone on a large Maple tree that lay across the back end of her vintage Mustang, the trunk crushed, the beautiful wire rims flattened against the ground.

Her heart stopped then sped up and her breath

came in short, painful gasps. Alex spun in a circle. Unleashed screams and moans echoed in her head. After her mother's death, she'd put whatever spare time and unspent emotion she had left into that car. The Mustang was solid and strong, something no one should have been able to take from her. But she of all people should've known better—life didn't come with guarantees.

She wrapped her arms tightly around her waist, plopped to the wet ground, and buried her face in her hands. Tears streamed between her fingers as huge, heartbreaking sobs shook her shoulders. When the distressing sound of anguish vibrated in her ears, her head popped up. She brushed her face against her shirt and was relieved that no one was paying any attention. They were too busy clearing away the brush and limbs. She was alone.

She swiped at the tears as a flash of green caught her attention. Her gaze moved from her tattered tent and wind-scattered clothes to a spot on the chain link fence. Resting her elbows on her knees, she recognized her lime green bra tangled in the fence.

No car, no tent, no clothes and no cowboy to love me, but my lime green bra survived.

Hysterical laughter bubbled from deep inside as a hand brushed across her back.

"Alex? Oh my God. Are you okay?" Shellie moaned. "Look at your car! Oh Alex. Alex? Alex! Are you listening to me?"

She tried to muffle her frenzied laughter with her hand as her friend dropped down beside her.

Shellie shook her shoulders. "What? What are you laughing at? This is awful!"

Alex pulled her hand from mouth and pointed to the fence.

"What is that? Is that your favorite br...B-R-A," her friend stammered just before breaking into a fit of laughter.

Alex brushed the tears from her eyes and caught her breath, only to lose it again when Shellie pointed to the bright green bra and let lose another bellyful of giggles.

The merriment burned out like a shooting star, a bright flash then nothingness. She stared at Shellie who stared back. Sawing, cutting and voices rose around them, but they were silent.

Alex's throat tightened, and she had to force out words. "Oh, Shellie. This weekend has been nothing but bad luck. I just want to sit here and cry—but I can hear my mom's voice, 'count your blessings.'" She wrapped her arms around the world's best friend. "We're lucky neither one of us was here when the storm came through. I've got you, a new project with the Mustang to fix, and a whole lot less to pack..." A giggle burst from her chest.

"All right, then." Shellie slapped her knee and broke up the moment. "Let's see if we can find anything to wear besides a lime green bra."

Alex stood up slowly. "A dry jacket or a pair of pants would be nice right about now." Eyes focused on the ground, she started the fashion hunt with the starlet.

"Alex?"

The deep voice was like a hot knife through butter. She spun around. Ben's brown eyes smoldered as he frowned. He was so handsome in a flannel shirt and denim jeans, her fingers ached to reach out and beg him to hold her.

He stepped in front of her. Thoughts flashed back causing her cheeks to burn as she recalled his Jack Daniels laced kisses and the strength of his arms around her. *Had he ever wanted me just for me?*

She shook her head and pushed the memories aside. He didn't want her. Pain stabbed through her heart but she managed to flash a shaky smile. "Hey, I hope you don't mind if I hang onto your shirt a little longer. As you can see"—she opened her arms wide—"it might be the only thing I have left."

He gave a dismissive wave, his smile entirely too sexy. "Keep the shirt, consider it yours."

When he stepped forward, she shook her head and shuffled back. Too much had happened, too many emotions were running through her head and heart—one stronger than all the rest. As much as she wanted him, she wasn't going to settle for less than true love. Without that, it was best to keep her distance.

"Alex, please," he whispered. "We've had too many misunderstandings this weekend. Just let me say this one thing..."

She nodded, crossing her arms tight over his shirt, holding in her emotions and wounded pride.

He lifted an arm toward her then wisely dropped it. "Alex, my emotions aren't like a buffet table, sympathy in this bowl, concern in this dish, passion on a platter. I'm more like a stew; everything is all mixed together." His hands mimicked his words and ended up pressed against his own chest. "Yes, I am sorry about your losses and your grief. At the same time, I'm drawn to you, and it's not pity that makes me want to hold you, touch you, kiss you. I can't separate my feelings, but at the same time—"

"Hey," someone from the crowd shouted. "It's a cowboy hat."

Alex stiffened.

Alex turned and her body stiffened at the sight of the tan Stetson. She whipped back around. "I know this looks bad, your hat ending up at my campsite, but I can explain—"

Ben reached for her hand. "Alex, it's okay."

She stepped back. If she returned the hat, at

least she could claim to have done one thing right this weekend. Alex turned and stopped; her heart fluttered. The kisses and dance hadn't been bad. Joy bubbled. *Buffet table, what in the world was he talking about?*

Alex closed her eyes to clear her head. With everything going on, she couldn't get her brain to catch up with what her body was feeling. Her body had a mind of its own, and a chemistry that matched Ben's perfectly. She opened her eyes and gulped air. The raw, uncensored emotion in Ben's eyes had her turning away.

A beam of light framed Ben's hat, and her heart raced. As if the light cleared a path in her unruly mind, her breath caught at sudden dawning. *What is wrong with me?* This is what she had dreamt of, her cowboy looking as Ben just did, like he wanted to crush her in his arms and never let her go.

The light of truth melted the fear in her heart and she smiled. All this time she had been focused on returning the Stetson, but this was much more than a hat. *This is my life, genuine feelings for an actual man, this man.*

"Miss?" An old gentleman waved the hat. "Does this belong to you, too, then?"

"Sure does." She stepped closer to the gentleman and held out a shaky hand.

With a small, crooked smile, the man passed the Stetson over and cocked his head toward the car. "One out of two ain't bad."

She winked. "Actually, it's two out of three and thank you."

Ben's eyes were partially obscured by his heavy lids. He looked tired. *The weekend had taken a toll on him, too.* She glanced down at the hat and brushed a speck from the brim. "The hat looks damn good considering everything it went through." She held out the Stetson. "It seems I'm destined to forever be returning your hat."

His fingers brushed hers as he accepted the hat. A jolt of electricity raced from his skin to hers. The chainsaws roared to life drowning out Ben's words.

"What?" Alex mouthed.

He pulled her to him and kissed her with a furor of passion.

Before she could wrap her arms around him, he stepped back and motioned in the direction of the men.

Alex bit her lip and nodded. He obviously needed to get back to helping the others. What do you say in a moment like this? The words, 'Don't go, please wait,' caught in her throat, and she swallowed them before they slipped between her parted lips. Her arms folded tight against her chest, she pressed her thighs tight together, the ache unbelievable.

He put the hat on his head.

Her fingers brushed her bottom lip.

The corner of his lip twitched up, and he strode toward the men.

The further he went, the larger the ache grew within her.

The saws continued to roar, and a moment later, Alex watched Ben and the others pull pieces of the tree from her car.

Shellie shouted into her ear. "I found a couple of dry things to wear. We can go back to the concert bowl and try to find rides in the morning."

Alex didn't want to leave. Didn't Shellie see, Ben had kissed her. She couldn't leave now. But she couldn't put into words what she was feeling to herself let alone her best friend. She wanted Ben, needed him...loved him.

Shellie's arm went around her shoulder, and Alex's legs went into motion as her friend propelled her forward.

A million should haves, could haves, bounced in

her brain as her feet took her further away from the man she loved.

She started to remember what Ben had said earlier about his emotional buffet, and the corners of her mouth stretched into a huge smile. *Oh! That's what he meant about his goofy buffet of emotions.* She'd been so sure about what she *thought* he felt or didn't feel, that she never paid attention to what he was trying to say. Ben was a far more complex man than Alex had given him credit for.

Like an engine without a battery, her thoughts had been grinding around, accomplishing nothing. But when she hooked up her heart and was in tune with her whole body, heart and soul, she was humming and running. Ben was part of the equation. Alex knew when they were together he could feel the chemistry, too. Her feet skipped along, barely touching the ground, her smile so wide her cheeks crinkled her eyes.

She couldn't believe she had misread pity for compassion. Had she always been too quick to judge?

Was it her own fear of falling in love that had prevented her from allowing anyone to get that close?

She could almost hear her mother whisper in her ear, *Second chances don't come along for everyone.*

She needed to get back to Ben...and Shellie was leading her the wrong way.

Alex twisted away from her friend and hoped for a miracle, but they were a long way from their campsite already. She had been so lost in her own head and heart that she didn't realize how far they'd walked.

"What?" Shellie asked, keeping a firm grasp on her arm and tugging her along with her.

The generators hummed and everything seemed to glow in the dimmed lights. "I need...I want..."

Alex dug in her heels, hoping to slow her friend down.

But Shellie didn't slow down; she just kept pushing Alex past the people who had taken refuge in the areas around the stage. They moved further into the concert bowl.

Weary eyes barely noticed them as they passed by the tables of campers who were huddled together on chairs and spoke in voices generally reserved for church services or championship golf games.

Her friend pushed her toward the permanent bathrooms housed in the pole barn to the far right of the stage.

Alex shook her head. "No, I have to—"

"You have to get warm and dry is what you have to do," the starlet ordered. Shellie dropped the backpack on the cement floor and pulled out a sweatshirt and shorts for Alex. "Here, put these on. I couldn't find any jeans."

Reluctantly, Alex did as she was told. Her damp, muddy, white pants landed on the floor as her fingers reached for the dry, semi-clean clothes. She slid into the shorts and pulled the sweatshirt over Ben's shirt. Her hands slid into her pockets, and her fingers brushed across a piece of paper. When she pulled it out, she recognized the scrawled handwriting.

"What do you have there?" her friend asked.

"Patrick's number," she practically shouted. Ben's friend. Ben would return to his campsite at some point. "We can't leave without saying good-bye."

Shellie yanked her cell phone from her pocket and shook her head. "Battery's dead."

"We'll walk. Come on. Let's go." She tugged on her friend's arm.

"Okay." Shellie hoisted up her backpack.

Alex rushed them across the familiar path to

their campground. There were no guards at the check points, and when they came to the fork in the road, they veered to the right up the gravel road. Alex's heart slammed against her ribs. Her brain fumbled to come up with the words to say. *Can I call you? When can I see you again?* Everything sounded so contrived. Her palms grew damp and her lips dry.

"Hey." Shellie pointed. "They didn't get any storm damage?"

The tents and trailers dotted along the road looked unscathed with only a sprinkling of a few leaves and some wet ground to show the rain had blown through.

Like love, Alex pushed her hands into her pockets. *For some, the all-consuming emotion brings destruction, and for others, the showers bring flowers and rainbows. For me, the winds brought a cowboy and hat.* She grinned at her suddenly philosophical musings.

They walked another block in silence, came to the school bus converted to a camper and took a left. After a few feet, Alex spotted Ben, the famed cowboy hat on his head. Patrick stood beside him; they watched the flames lick the logs of a small campfire, oblivious to the women watching them.

The muscles in Alex's neck tightened, and she couldn't even swallow. Her feet became rooted to the ground. Instead of charging into his arms and feeling the heat of their embrace, she stood trying to produce enough spit to swallow. Her mouth was so dry her upper lip stuck to her teeth.

"Hello," Shellie called out with both her arms waving like she was trying to land a jet airplane.

"Hot dang," Patrick yelled as he danced forward. "My two favorite women." He moved closer and winked. "Knew you wouldn't be able to stay away."

Ben rushed forward. His gaze swept over Alex. "Is everything okay?"

Finally, she managed to wedge her tongue between her lip and teeth to get some words out. "Yeah, we're fine. I just...I was thinking..."

A scream erupted and stopped Alex in mid-sentence.

The door to a large RV flung open and banged loudly against the siding. Julia swaggered out.

Ben stepped protectively in front of Alex, and she peeked over his shoulder at the hellion headed toward them. A white strip of tape crossed Julia's nose, her face was puffy and her eyes were glazed over.

Alex's shoulders sagged as her gaze bounced between Ben and the woman. *Great.* All she needed right now was to be taken back to jail. If she was more like Shellie, she would have planned for the unexpected and had her name and number written out; she could have slipped Ben the piece of paper before poor timing and bad luck found her yet again.

"Cowboy," Julia warned as she moved toward him. "She's not staying."

Ben narrowed his eyes. "Alex and Shellie *are* staying."

Alex hadn't even realized she was holding her breath until the air whistled through her parched lips.

Julia sashayed to him, placed her palms on his waist, seductively brushed her chest against him and began to sniffle. "After what she did to me?"

He put his hands on Julia's shoulder and pushed her away. "She didn't punch you and she didn't steal the hat."

Julia stumbled. "I heard you tell Patrick the hat was by her tent. That's proof...see, I told you—"

In a heart-clenching and very unexpected movement, Ben turned and placed the hat on Alex's head.

"The hat belongs to Alex. I gave it to her last

year."

Julia stared wide-eyed at Ben, then Alex, and back again. Huffing a harsh sound of disbelief, she staggered back to the RV.

Ben reached for Alex. His fingers brushed her forearm. "I'm sorry. I never should have allowed Julia to talk that way to you. She never should have even come on this trip."

Alex gloried in the feel of his hands on her again, but hesitated to let herself want too much too soon. She searched for the answers in his liquid brown eyes. Was he giving her the hat as an ending...or a beginning?

Shellie squealed. Alex whipped her head around in time to see a golf cart skid to a stop beside them. A split second later, her friend was in the front seat with her arms wrapped around Joe. *They make loving look so simple and easy.*

Her friend grabbed Joe by the shoulders and planted a loud, noisy kiss on his lips and a couple of pecks on his cheek before exiting the car. She raced from the cart to Patrick and almost knocked him over as she wrapped him in a bear hug. "Thanks for everything."

Ben extended his hand to Shellie. "It was nice to meet you."

"A pleasure, sort of." She clasped his hand. "Come on, Alex," she added, bumping her shoulder. "Joe offered us a place to stay. Hurry up and say your goodbyes."

Alex's heart raced as Patrick moved closer and Ben moved back.

"Yeah, Alex, hurry up and kiss me," Patrick teased.

Ben's arm halted him mid-stride. "Alex, why don't you stay here? We've got plenty of room."

"Oh, but..." Shellie trailed off, her gaze focused on Ben. Then her friend's right eyebrow hopped up and down as a smirk slid over her face and she winked, shrugged and smiled bright as Hollywood all at the same time. "Of course, why not. Joe said the place was *real* small so you'd probably be more comfortable here?"

Shellie was one of a kind. Alex wrapped her arms around her best friend.

"Here's your chance," her friend whispered. "Clearly there is something going on between you."

"But I don't know what to do." Alex whispered back honestly.

"Your heart will know what to do." Shellie gave her a little push. "I'll be back in the morning. Bye." She jogged back to the cart with her arms waving.

Patrick mumbled something about not getting kissed and disappeared into the dark.

Alex turned and found Ben right behind her. He caught her arm and she gave a quiet gasp at the little pinpricks of shockwaves. The area was so quiet she could hear their hearts pounding as their gazes locked.

His hot palm came up to brush her cool cheek as the fingers of his other hand tangled in her hair, pulling her closer.

"Wasn't that some storm?" Alex asked.

Ben's hand left her cheek to wrap her in a bear hug. His chest and belly rumbled against hers as he laughed and squeezed her tight. "Yeah, quite a storm."

Her arms slid around his waist, and they remained toe-to-toe long after the mutual laughter ended. Alex soaked up the moment. His arms, his scent, his breath surrounding her, holding her, hugging her. His lips brushed the top of her forehead, and she was as content as a lazy cat slowly twitching her tail while lying in the sun.

Strong, warm hands framed her face as his lips lowered to hers. Her eyelids fluttered shut. The heat and intensity increased as the kiss deepened. Her heart raced, and a shiver went through her. The night had turned cold but it wasn't the air that caused her limbs to tremble. She was scared. Emotionally, she had never been this far before. In a kiss, she tried to convey all the emotions she held for this man.

Ben's lips drew away. "You're cold." He steered her toward the fire and nuzzled her neck. "Wait here. I'll get you something warm to wear."

By the time he came back with a blue-and-white flannel shirt her knees were knocking together.

He slipped her arms through the shirt and stood behind her, his arms wrapped tightly around her. "I enjoy sharing my clothes with you." His intimate words caressed her ear.

The campfire warmed the front of her as Ben's radiating body heat warmed her back. Lazy Sunday mornings parading around in nothing but Ben's shirt flashed like commercials through her mind. The thought of his hands slipping off all those Sunday morning shirts was like a flame to dry kindling; her body went from smoldering to smokin' hot.

He turned her around. They were chest to chest. His arms wrapped around her waist. "I want you."

The words she had longed to hear surrounded her heart like his shirt surrounded her body. Second chances. She was lucky enough to get one, and she was going to grasp on tight.

Through the thickness of her emotions and raging hormones, all Alex could do was murmur her consent.

She melted as his hands slid lower to the small of her back. His grip tightened, and she was pulled closer. His tongue traced the outline of her lips. Their mouths danced and her heart soared. A sensation between a tingle and jolt crested in the pit of her stomach. Her knees weakened as his kiss sang through her veins.

She could tell by the intensity of the desire in his eyes that he was following where his heart led. Alex swallowed against the power of his gaze. *It was one thing to daydream and quite another to hold the dream.*

"I want..." his voice cracked.

Her mouth smothered his last words as she gave him a slow, tantalizing kiss, and her worries scattered like colorful leaves on an autumn breeze. Orange and yellow flames flickered, and the night became magical for both of them. They were in this together. For the first time in this torrid weekend, she was reading him loud and clear...and also reading herself. This night was only the beginning.

Their mouths melted together, his fingers tangled in her hair, and her hands clutched his shoulders to pull him closer.

She wanted him to remove his flannel shirt, the one he had moments before placed on her so gently. She yearned to feel his touch and caress on her bare skin.

Her hips rocked and his hands slipped to the small of her waist. His finger found her flesh and sent shivers of delight up her spine. She was shocked to discover the soft moans she heard were her own. He was taking her with him to a place beyond her wildest imagination.

His teasing kisses trailed across her cheek. "Your skin is so soft." He rocked them back and forth. "You feel perfect in my arms."

Her hands slipped under his shirt, and his muscles danced beneath her touch. His lips trailed kisses across her jaw. He nuzzled her neck as his hand found her breast. She sighed and caught her breath.

The air rushed from her lungs, her body tingled,

and her head spun. She clung to him like he was a lifeline. He was the one who could save her, protect her and allow her to love again.

"You're shivering." He moved away slightly. "Let's stand closer to the fire."

Fear crept back into her head. She was afraid of losing, of making a mistake. The more she thought, the colder she became, and when she shivered, she realized her brain couldn't keep her warm, only her heart could. If she couldn't trust her heart she'd never be warm again. *What more does this cowboy have to do to convince me he loves me? I know he does, my body knows he does but my head...*

She stepped back.

"What?" He stared at his empty arms.

"I-I can't." The words cracked from her tight throat. The cost for taking a chance on love was a gut-wrenching, stabbing pain that would subside to a raw, throbbing ache if she gambled and lost. She wasn't sure if she could pay the price.

Her body wanted to give in to the sensations, to accept the bliss his lips and arms offered. She reasoned, *no one's guaranteed tomorrow, take pleasure where you can.* Her heart argued the greater the love, the deeper the pain, walk away now while you can. She looked into the depth of his eyes.

She buried her face into his neck. "I'm scared of losing one more thing."

"Hey." He lifted her chin gently to look in her eyes. "I don't want to get hurt either, but sometimes you have to take a chance. Last year I found the woman of my dreams, and in a flash, she was gone."

She swallowed hard. "That woman doesn't exist." She stepped back from his arms.

"That's okay. Everyone's life changes after a tragedy."

Alex held her manicured hands in front of his face. "She never existed. Shellie bought the dress and this weekend, the hair, nails, make-up are all pretend. I'm a grease monkey, Ben. I change oil for a living. I love working on cars and..."

His hands rested on her shoulders. "It's not the clothes you wear, or what's under your nails. I don't care if your fingers are stained with oil, manure, or ink. I love you, Alex, not because you are beautiful, sexy...and now I realize as a bonus can fix a car, too." He chuckled and pulled her tight. "You are sincere, honest, kind, smart and funny. I want to hold you in my arms and never let you go. I love the way you touch me, laugh and care. I want to learn everything about you. Trust me, pleas—"

"Stop. Did you just say you love me?" Her heart went into overdrive.

"Did you just miss the best speech I've ever given to a woman? And I wasn't even finished." He grinned down at her. "Yes, I said I love you and I am so glad you got stuck on those words. At least I know you were listening to part of what I was saying."

Jokingly aghast, Alex went to punch Ben, but he grabbed her arm, and they stumbled over a chair and tumbled to the ground. Alex landed sprawled against Ben's chest.

"Hmmmm, you like it on top," he teased.

She tried to get up but his arms held her in place.

"Can't you see, Alex. We are both at the same place. The place of wonder. Wonder what he thinks, wonder what she means. It's the way of men and women, but I can promise you one thing—I want you to spend years wondering about me, and I will spend years wondering about you."

"I wi—wish—I wish..." she stuttered, full of his heartfelt confession.

"Shh, it's okay." He pulled her tight. "I wish I could promise you a future with no pain, but I can't. Besides, I'd rather have a night of perfect bliss and risk pain, rather than a lifetime of mediocre and not knowing. We are perfect together and shouldn't waste one second of the time we're given." He nuzzled her neck. "But the time doesn't start ticking until we get to the tent. My backside is getting wet."

Alex laughed as she stood to let Ben get up. The moment he was upright, her fingers trailed over his chest, and she planted kisses around his neck.

A murmur vibrated from him as he clutched the back of her thighs and pressed her tight up against him. Ben's hands moved over her body like she was the wallpaper, and he was the wall. His hands didn't stop until there wasn't an air pocket left between the two of them.

"Tell me I'm not dreaming," he murmured low.

She pressed her lips to his.

"Alex," he said between kisses. "I really do love you and I don't know what I've done to deserve a second chance—"

She kissed his words with her lips. Their hearts beat in unison. Her eyes slid shut and she gave herself up to the desire burning in her soul.

Ben was right. She no longer wanted to be someone who danced outside the fire; she wanted to be the one to know for sure, the one willing to risk it all.

"I love you, too," she said as tears of joy streamed down her face.

"Then may I have this dance, forever?" Ben asked.

Her lips stretched into a wide, tear-stained smile. "Yes."

And they danced.

Epilogue

Alex couldn't believe how fast a year could go by as she once again stood on the campgrounds of Country Time.

Her grin widened to the size of a child's on Christmas morning when the sounds of country music blared and voices shouted around her.

Her heart beat faster at the site of Ben bent over the tent.

He stood up and glanced over his shoulder. "Hey, what are you going to do? Spend the day looking at the sights?"

She smile and nodded.

"All right," he smiled back. "But I do expect you to reward me later on with..."

Her eyebrow rose. "I'll do better than that."

With a growl, he rushed toward her, wrapping his arms about her waist and twirling her faster and faster. Their lips melted together.

"Hey, you two. Knock it off," Patrick called out. "At the rate you're going, by the time you get your tent set up, it'll be time to take it down."

They ignored him and continued their kiss. There'd be time later for setting up camp.

The horn of a golf cart blared and Alex twisted in Ben's arms. "Shellie!" she shouted.

Ben kissed her forehead and released her. Alex rushed to her friend as Shellie bolted from the cart waving a pink bag.

"You'll never believe what I bought you."

She laughed, wondering what she'd find this

year beneath the pink tissue. She ignored the present to hug her friend. Between school and Ben, she'd found little time to visit with Shellie beyond telephone and email.

"It's so good to see you!" Shellie ended the hug and pushed the bag toward Alex.

"Hi, Shellie," Ben said as he walked over. "What do you have there?"

Alex's cheeks heated as her hand crinkled the paper.

"Hurry up," Shellie urged. "Show him."

Alex pulled out a turquoise bra and matching thong. Attached to the two items was a note that she read aloud. "They match the maid-of-honor dress I'm asking you to wear—*oh my gosh*," Alex yelled in excitement.

Shellie flashed a diamond ring in front of her face. "Does this mean you'll be my maid of honor?"

"Of course! Yes! When did this happen?" she asked, grabbing her friend's hand.

"Congratulations." Ben wrapped his arms around both of them. "I'm going to let you two catch up while I finish putting up the tent," he said, dropping a kiss on Alex's head.

The sun had set by the time she'd caught up on all the details with Shellie. Their group moved slowly to the VIP campgrounds. Alex couldn't be happier. Shellie was getting married and she was going to be the maid of honor. She grinned and hooked her arms through Ben and Shellie's arms as music from the karaoke stage drifted on the sweet summer breeze.

She leaned into Ben; the weight of his arm around her shoulder had become a contented constant. With her college only a twenty-minute drive from his family farm, they found themselves together more than apart. He helped with her studies, she helped him with his chores, occasionally they did maintenance on a family vehicle.

They swayed to the music coming from the karaoke speakers. His lips brushed the top of her head. "Wait here," Ben said.

He headed to the front of the stage. *I'll never get tired of watching the way he fills out those faded blue jeans.* Cute little butt, long lean muscular legs, worn cowboy boots kicking up bits of sand. He was perfect.

She watched him hand a slip of paper to the man emceeing the event.

"What's he doing?" Shellie asked.

Alex shrugged. Her eyes locked with Ben's and a million butterfly wings fluttered in her stomach.

Unexpectedly, he climbed on stage. He flashed a smile and swiped his palms across the thighs of his jeans before grabbing the microphone. "I'd like to sing this song to Alex. She hasn't said, 'yes', yet, because I haven't asked so keep your fingers crossed for me because later tonight, I'm hoping to be the happiest man here."

Her heart stopped, and her knees went weak, but Ben's voice was strong as he began to sing Rascal Flatt's, *Bless the Broken Road.*

She listened to every word and brushed tears of joy from her cheek. When the last note faded into the silent night, a sea of hands with fingers crossed filled the air.

Unable to wait, she met him half way from the stage.

Ben dropped to bended knee. "Will you marry me?"

"Yes." Her voice was strained with emotion. Shivers of joy rushed through her as Ben took hold of her shaking hand and swiftly stood.

He swept Alex into his embrace. "She said, 'yes,'" he yelled out joyously just before kissing her soundly to the cheers and hollers from the crowd.

Other Wild Rose Press Titles by Christine Columbus

Christmas Mischief
A flat tire on a cold, snowy afternoon, and the tall, dark, handsome stranger who stops to help doesn't ask for your phone number.

Uncle Mike's Love
After twelve years away from his hometown, Mike is back in town to take care of his nephews and hoping to get a second chance with Patty.

Coffee And Love To Go
Dan finds he is the topic of conversation on a women's talk show about meaningful glances, thanks to a beautiful woman with red hair.

A Hard Day On The Farm
Molly moved to the country, met neighbor George, and learned to drive the tractor—just one aspect of farm life Molly found enjoyable.

First Class Male
Did Mark bestow more than his mother's dog? Will Michelle's unexpected pet bring more than drama into her life?

Drama Queen
Did Mark bestow more than his mother's dog? Will Michelle's unexpected pet bring more than drama into her life?

Happy Meal
Mark suspected his notoriously stubborn mother was up to something but never guessed their weekly dinners out would end up as they did.

Lost
Sometimes getting lost isn't a recipe for disaster, but a path to happiness.

A word from the author...

I have many stories to tell about some of my favorite men. The men are all devastatingly gorgeous, have flawless, toned, hard bodies and a naturally charismatic presence, and as far as I know all the perfect men in my stories are fictional, but you never know. I am an optimist.

I have lived my entire life in Minneapolis, Minnesota. I have been published in creative non-fiction, poetry and children's fiction stories. When I first began writing I eagerly shared those stories with my daughter and son, but when I began writing romance I hid my works from their eyes and soon the kids began to tell tales about me writing XXX rated material.

I have been a member of Midwest Fiction Writers and Romance Writers of America since 2002. I have taken numerous writing classes because I like to know that someone is reading my writing, even if it is just the instructor.

My favorite comment from a teacher was Patrick at the University of Iowa who wrote that he looked forward to reading my work because I was a glitter of gold in a box of sand.

You can contact Christine at
ChristineColumbus@msn.com

Check out Christine's blog!

CPSIA information can be obtained at www.ICGtesting.com
2296151.V00001B/68/P